THE PASSAGE AT MOOSE BEACH

THE PASSAGE AT MOOSE BEACH

MICHAEL FOSTER
ART BY GLORIA MILLER ALLEN

Z GIRLS PRESS

This book may be ordered in bulk, discount pricing available for schools, non-profits, and educational organizations.

Contact publisher at
www.CallingCardBooks.com

Art by Gloria Miller Allen

Designed and Published by Z Girls Press
www.ZGirlsPress.com
Sacramento, California

First Edition
Copyright © 2018 by Michael Foster
www.MichaelsCabinBooks.com

ISBN-13:978-0-9965683-6-4

This book is dedicated to wildland firefighters everywhere.

Without their courage, dedication, extraordinary efforts, and the sacrifices they make, this book would not exist. They are true heroes, and with climate change, are more important than ever.

Wildland Firefighter Foundation's main focus is to help families of firefighters killed in the line of duty and to assist injured firefighters and their families.

WILDLAND FIREFIGHTEF FOUNDATIO

www.wffoundation.org

2049 Airport Way
Boise, ID 83705

We honor and acknowledge past, present, and future members of the wildland firefighting community, and partner with private and interagency organizations to bring recognition to wildland firefighters.

5% of Author royalties will be donated to this wonderful organization for the life of the book.

For Valeria who inspired me,
for Sabrina who changed me,
and for my mom and dad
who gave all this to me.

CONTENTS

PROLOGUE

Did she actually turn enemies into friends and watch in anguish as a mountain crumbled before her? The memories are a bit foggy now. But looking back, Alicia could only wonder if it all really happened. Did she actually step through a barrier at that small beach, and enter another realm? If she did, it was a place mixed with equal amounts of wonder and terror. Or did she simply lose her footing in the pouring rain, fall, and hit her head on an old log or a huge rock? She supposed it was possible that *maybe* it was all just a delusion. Perhaps someday, Alicia would know the truth.

One would never guess just by looking at it, but there was magic in this place. That unassuming patch of sand on an otherwise overgrown lake shore. You could float by it a dozen times, or meander by in a boat trolling for rainbow trout that love to hide in the lake weeds. *Darn, another snag!* Or maybe just be on the lake to get a summer glow on your skin and never see it. If by chance it did catch your eye, it might not stick in your mind. Instead, it could just become a blend of all the beauty of the lake. However, if the time of day was just right, if the sunlight filtered through the trees just so, and your curious mind was looking, maybe, just maybe, you would become one of the lucky few.

The locals knew this place. From the far side of the lake, it was often possible to see one of the majestic forest creatures coming to the shoreline for a drink or a quick cooldown. On those warm, lazy days of summer, the moose would wander into the water from that beach and stand at a depth of five feet or so, feeding on the tall grasses and water lilies that sprouted from the surface of the lake--hence the name. Their large backs and shoulders were still visible above the surface due to their tremendously long legs. Sometimes, if you looked closely, you might see the smaller stature of a calf accompanying the parent. And if the mood struck, you might take the rowboat over and get a closer look at them--but not too close. Making the journey across the water when the beach was empty, actually making landfall and stepping out onto that shoreline, well friends, that is not the end of the journey but just the beginning.

CH. I THE LAKE IN THE WOODS

The lake was a beautiful place which measured about a mile in width and two in length, just big enough to water ski on during warm afternoons. Fishing was a popular activity and kids would give it a go in the day so that parents could enjoy their afternoons free from worry about what the children were up to. Then when evening rolled around, fathers would gather their tackle boxes, head out in their rowboats, and take their turn at fly fishing, trying to get those "famous trout" when the fish were more active, feeding on the insects dancing across the surface of the water.

Alicia was an adventurous sixth grader, a young girl who cherished spending summer months at the lake with her mother and father at their family's cabin. She was a natural-born swimmer and loved to snorkel near the shoreline to watch the minnows, pollywogs, and other interesting things not visible from the rowboat. They would flit through the shallows in their jerky, seemingly random, movements. And then there were the dark spaces, pockets of blackness right near the shore underneath some bush hanging into the water, or behind a large rock. Alicia knew where all those were, and she would swim just a little bit farther away from those spots to not disturb them. In her vivid imagination, she never knew what might be hiding in those dark nooks and crannies!

Years ago, Alicia's kindergarten teacher created an "ocean in a bottle" for the class, bringing a five-gallon container filled with murky lake water for them to observe. That was when Alicia realized for the first time just how many living things called the lake she and her parents swam in "home," and she had been fascinated ever since.

She loved watching nature, but when an insect stopping for a drink on the lake's surface became lunch for the trout, she shuddered feeling bad for the little creepy-crawly and had to remind herself that is the way nature works. There were times when she was small that she would shoo the trout and sucker fish away from the minnows that she thought of as her friends. Now that she was older, she understood the circle of life better and, while it still bothered her, she allowed nature to take its course.

Nestled in a small valley just outside the quaint town of Cascade, Idaho, in the Boise National Forest, the west shore of the lake was lined with docks. They were barely visible from the water and were the only clue to the cabins hidden behind the trees. Where the highway came in from town, you could find campgrounds aplenty, and on weekdays when they were empty, Alicia loved to wander through and explore, maybe finding a trinket or treasure some camper had left behind as they packed up their cars to return home. Alicia knew where the Jerusalem crickets liked to hide under old rotten logs, and where she got the best view of the scampering squirrels that swarmed the camping sites each weekend as a new batch of tourists came with delicious snacks. She never understood why some folks preferred the big lodge perched on the north shore and "camped" with a roof over their heads, when it was so much more interesting to spend the night outdoors! Even though her family had a cabin, on those occasions when the nights were warm, they would set up a tent in the small clearing and enjoy a night of "roughing it."

To the east and south, the shoreline was undeveloped, with pine trees and bushes coming right up to the water's edge. It would remain that way—everyone hoped so anyway. The only walking paths were those created by the myriad of creatures who called the forest home. Alicia and her father kept a laminated tracking card in the top kitchen drawer. It showed all the paw prints and hoof-prints of the many animals that lived in the forest. Every year, it was a tradition for them to do some "old fashioned tracking" around the cabin, and at dinner on the first night, report to her mother what wildlife the family might see this year.

The mountains around the lake were snow-kissed until late June. None of them were particularly tall, except for the peak to the northeast. If you looked closely, there was a tiny shape of a lookout tower, perched high so that the fire watcher could keep a sharp eye out for forest fires. The mountains' shapes were almost like sometime long ago, giants passing by decided to lie down for a nap and never woke up. Maybe they got tired from walking, or maybe they were just enjoying Mother Nature's artistry. Over the years, trees and bushes covered the giants' rocky skin creating a brilliant landscape of green. Maybe they are still sleeping to this day, waiting for just the right magic to awaken them.

Summers were warm, with temperatures reluctantly climbing from the 60s and 70s in June, until August when the mercury pushed much higher. Alicia also kept her own special weather notebook in that same top kitchen drawer. Now that she was older, Alicia told her parents that she was going to figure out if the animal tracks, the amount of mountain snow, and lake level were at all connected to the prints that they saw. She absolutely loved science, especially earth science, so making notes in her weather book was something she looked forward to every visit to the cabin.

Dusk was often downright cold, perfect for building a fire and watching the colors dance. Thunderstorms were a semi-regular occurrence, with the rain hitting hard and occasional bursts of hail sounding like stones clattering against the roof. Thunder echoed around the valley as if those giants had decided to wake up and roar with all their might. August into September were the best months when days were perfect for swimming, hiking, and just enjoying the fun of being there. It was hard for a kid to hang around the house. If you were lucky, your family could extend cabin time until mid-October. Watching the colors changing from green to beautiful shades of orange and brown was something that could not be explained--it had to be experienced. When you felt snow in the air, it was almost time to head home.

The winter months were mostly quiet up there, with cabins standing empty and frozen. Owners could not wait to return to warmer climates when the sounds of the forest were muffled by the cotton-like drifts of snow. The lodge remained open year-round to accommodate the tried and true hunters and snowmobilers. It was the sole refuge for visitors willing to brave the slick mountain roads. Snow would pile up to six feet high, closing roads to regular vehicles around the lower end of the lake. The water would freeze over enough to allow snowmobiles to traverse its surface. Intrepid ice fishermen were often on the lake near the lodge, ice drills resting by their sides. They always had a Thermos of strong, black coffee, or a flask of whiskey on hand to warm their insides while their faces froze.

Time was an interesting thing at the lake.

It played tricks on the mind. Days could stretch forever which was a blessing, because at the end of any visit, in hindsight, the stay always seemed too short. Even the sun was reluctant to leave this place. It often lingered in the sky, its final rays clinging to the treetops until they could no longer deny the laws of physics. It can't be bedtime already? was the standard argument while battling a yawn. But the sun just went down, was a common complaint heard by parents.

Was this distortion of time just an optical illusion of the mind? An Escher-esque rendition of how time works. Or maybe, just maybe, the tiniest bit of magic from the beach was leaking into our world. After all, there was powerful and ancient magic at work.

Thinking that special enchanted force could, or would, be contained might be considered foolish.

CH. 2 SECRETS TO FIND

There was no trail too boring, no pond too mundane, and no unknown that she would ignore. Alicia already knew where every special place was hidden within a mile radius of her family's cabin. She could not wait to find mysteries that were yet to be discovered.

The log structure was built in the early 1900s by her grandfather. Alicia would count the days until her family's visits to the mountains. Every year, when summer rolled around, the family would pack up their belongings quick as could be and set out on the drive to the cabin.

For Alicia, the "getting there" part was interminably long. Their family had moved out of the state before she was born due to her father's work, and now it took practically an entire day's drive to get there. Small town after small town passed by, with regular stops for food, gas, and restroom breaks. Long stretches of roads with boring scenery out the windows usually lulled her to sleep with their emptiness. She would rather dream about what she expected to see when they finally got there. Her family always brought a bag of snacks in the car so she could have an apple or some crackers if she wanted. And sometimes her mom would bring a book and read it out loud as the miles passed.

Her favorite part of the drive though, was the last thirty miles or so when they finally entered the forest. Alicia would roll down her car window, looking almost like a dog, sticking her nose out to inhale the scent of fresh pine. It was at that moment she knew they were close.

The cabin was just a single room which was all her family needed. It had two beds, a small kitchenette, a dining table, and a couch to curl up on and read a good book. The Old Mother West Wind series from Thornton W. Burgess was one of her favorites. The cozy fireplace always left the smell of wood smoke in the air and in her clothes. Alicia absolutely loved that smell. It was a constant reminder that this cabin and this place were her true home.

Winter months were a drag, but she mindfully did her school work which made her parents and teachers proud. She was a good student and liked school, but Alicia knew that the only place where she truly learned was at the cabin. She could tell you the names of a hundred varieties of plants and recognize dozens of birds from their distinctive songs. Not many kids her age listened to birds enough to do that, and her teachers were always surprised and amazed at how much Alicia knew. She could also describe, in great detail, the differences between a chipmunk and a squirrel (for starters, chipmunks have pointy noses). She could tell you the best places to look for huckleberries, which she always said were the bestest berries ever. That term was a carryover from when she was little, and it made her mom laugh when she used it, so she used it often. Alicia just loved those wild huckleberries, especially in her mom's pancakes.

She could also tell you the best places to hunt for toads: in the shallows next to the mossy rocks along the water. And garter snakes, which she could usually find in the grass or tree litter at the edge of the forest near the family dock. Her parents knew she would, no doubt, come home grinning and excited to show off her latest catch. Like it or not, her mother had to get used to having snakes and other not-so-loveable creatures around the house during their visits to the cabin.

Alicia's greatest love was exploration. She would climb to the tops of small hills and look out over the forest imagining how many secrets the entire thing could hold. Her special place was teeming with amazing things! Who knew what kind of caterpillar or salamander was hiding just out of her reach? In her mind, a jumble of rocks could be a ruined ogre castle. Alicia was absolutely convinced that at night, that small shallow of water just to the east, where tiny green frogs liked to congregate on warm days, turned into a fairy playground. She knew with all her heart that one day she would discover the most amazing secret of all. She just didn't know what that was yet, or how her life would change if she found it.

CH. 3 STEPPING IN

"Hey girls, it is so beautiful today. Let's take the boat and row over to the beach on the other side. The water is calm and it's the perfect day for a swim." Richard looked over at his daughter while his wife Katie washed and dried breakfast dishes. Alicia's father had made the most delicious biscuits and gravy from scratch, one of Alicia's favorite meals, and now she was resting comfortably with a full belly. "What do you say, kiddo?"

Richard's goal wasn't the big tourist beach to the north. He had pointed towards the small and unassuming beach straight out from their dock on the opposite, undeveloped side of the lake. The water was shallow there, even several feet from the shore. It was perfect for wading, splashing, and whatnot because it warmed so quickly in the sunshine. The best part of all was the temperature outside on this sunny day.

"I don't know, honey," Katie said cautiously as she looked to the southern skies. "The clouds that way look dark. You know how quickly the weather can change around here."

"Mom, I want to go!" yelled Alicia enthusiastically. "It's so warm outside, and it sounds perfect."

"It's true, Kate. I think we can get there, swim, and get back with plenty of time to spare. We may have some rain by tonight, but it is still a long way off."

"Well I don't trust it," Kate sounded dubious, "and I don't want it to start raining on MY head while we are coming home."

"Aww, Mom..."

"But if you two want to go, don't let me stop you. It's always good to have some father-daughter bonding time." She paused, holding a plate in one hand and a dish towel in the other. "Besides, I saw some new wildflowers starting to bloom out in the yard and I'd like to try and sketch them with the afternoon light." Alicia's mother had recently taken up drawing and she had a new set of colored pencils she was eager to try out. "So you go and enjoy yourselves. But sweetheart, please keep an eye on that sky and head straight home if you think you'll get caught out there in a downpour."

"Will do, honey."

"Thanks, Mom!"

"And don't forget your lifejackets!" she called through the open cabin door as Alicia and Richard headed toward the dock.

Rowing across the lake took about fifteen minutes, and Richard watched the sky most of the way. Alicia knew what was going on in that head of his. Her dad would hate it if her mom was right, but it wasn't too windy. The distant storm seemed to be parked right where it was, so neither father nor daughter felt the need to be concerned.

From a distance, the beach was nothing more than a speck. A tiny white patch bordered on both sides by endless green and the occasional brown of a fallen tree.

"I want to be a botanist when I grow up." The enthusiastic girl loved discussing her life plans with anyone who would listen to them.

Alicia felt that familiar gaze from Richard when her parents would say things like *Where did this small, intelligent creature, so filled with curiosity, imagination, and delight, come from?* She hated it when he talked to her like she was still a child. Her dad knew this but he could not contain himself during these special moments with her. Alicia was enjoying herself and hoped he would not get all sappy and emotional right now.

"A botanist, huh?" Richard was used to Alicia's ever-changing ideas about what she wanted to be when she grew up. After reading Jules Verne, she was going to be a marine biologist and invent a deep-sea submersible. That way, she could explore the deepest parts of the oceans to find exotic creatures.

"Yeah. Or maybe a forest ranger. I want to be able to explore this forest until I know it like the back of my hand."

Alicia's hand was trailing in the water as she gazed over the side of the boat looking for fish lurking just below the surface. They passed a water lily and she let the wide, green leaf slide through her fingers. A huge dragon-fly had been perched on the large yellow flower that stood above the pad, but it flitted away when Alicia's hand got too close. The bottom of the pad felt weirdly slimy, she thought.

Alicia knew that her father had spent many hours over the years exploring the lands around the cabin. He liked telling her it was at this very lake where he had first laid eyes upon his beautiful wife. He said Alicia reminded him of when he and Katie were teenagers and would play with other kids from the campground. Alicia liked playing tag and hide-and-go-seek just like her parents did. She also loved to invent games just like he said he used to, usually obscure and adventurous, concocted to fit the woodland setting. She would often ask her father to describe the kinds of games he invented and played them herself if she could. Most often, she liked her own inventions better.

Her father's time at the lake was all too brief back then. It was her mom's parents who owned the cabin. Her dad was only a tourist to this land. But for Alicia's family, a visit to the lake was an annual thing. Everyone knew her grandfather because he was a troop leader with the Boy Scouts and led camping expeditions around the lake. As part of the troop,

Richard learned many of the traditional skills, such as building a campfire, tying knots, and creating makeshift shelters. He told Alicia that his love of scouting vanished quickly once that first spark of love for the girl who would one day become his wife emerged. Richard's longing to return the following year, and the year after, only increased.

Alicia was only a few months old when she first visited the cabin, though, naturally, she had no clear memories of that herself. When she tried to recall them, the only thoughts she had were of the clear, vivid forest colors.

Her father would talk of her eyes being wide at all the sights, thoughtful and contemplative, even at that young age. Alicia would smile and giggle baby giggles when they would feed the squirrels peanuts right out of their hands. Richard would strap her in tight to the baby carrier and off they would go for short hikes on the nearby trails. Alicia appeared to thrive in the environment and Richard could not wait for her to be old enough for him to begin teaching her all of the fascinating things there were to see and learn there.

***

"Dad, did you hear me?" Spotting the shoreline of the beach, Alicia called out to her father, but he didn't respond.

"Oh sorry, honey, I was lost in thought."

"I said we are almost there."

Richard turned to look over his shoulder, and sure enough, the speck of beach had widened to a shore measuring about twelve feet across. He looked for a good space to tie up the boat so it would not drift away, yet far enough away to avoid bumping against the small rocks nearby.

Alicia stripped off her lifejacket and flung herself over the edge of the boat before it stopped moving. She was already prepared with her swim shorts and top on, so she wasn't wasting any time. At eleven years old, she was a strong swimmer, and the water here was barely two feet deep. Richard had no worries about accidents happening.

"Don't get too far away from shore until I can join you."

"Come on, Dad, I'm fine," Alicia said with impatience, moving further out into the water.

"I know you are, just let me act like the good parent I am supposed to be."

Richard finished securing the boat and then waded to the shore, enjoying the warm sand on his feet. Stripping off his shirt and tossing it aside along with a couple of towels, he stepped into the cool water to join his daughter who was, of course, ignoring his warning and proceeding to swim out as far as she could while still touching the bottom. Now was not the time to raise a fuss, and he knew she could handle herself. If she went under, which would not happen, he could get to her in seconds.

They swam and splashed in the water for what seemed like forever, their bodies became accustomed to the cold in no time. Richard would crouch down and have Alicia stand on his shoulders. She loved to clamber up, her wet feet slipping as they tried to gain a solid foothold on his wide shoulders. He would then thrust his legs to straighten them, sending his daughter flying through the air and landing with a splash several feet away. Bursting up from the water, she would laugh hysterically with joy. *Do it again, do it again*, she'd cheer.

And he would, over and over, until they were both exhausted. After that, it was just good to relax and feel the soft water caress their skin.

A drop of water landed on Richard's head, and he instinctively knew it did not come from the lake. Dreading what he was going to see, he looked to the sky and knew instantly that Katie had been right. The rain had arrived."Come on, Lish, let's get a move on. Maybe we can beat this storm home."

"Mom was right."

"Yeah, I know she was," he said with a somber, thoughtful look on his face, "And I know Kate's going to be standing there with that I-told-you-so look on her face."

"But we still had fun anyway, right?" Alicia said, slapping her hand on the water and watching the droplets intently to see if a rainbow showed itself to her.

"Definitely!"

Richard and Alicia slogged to the shore and quickly toweled off. Richard pulled on his shirt and moved to start freeing the boat from the log where he had secured it. It seemed in the years that passed since childhood, he had forgotten more about tying the perfect constrictor knot than he remembered. It was taking much longer than normal to undo it this time. Meanwhile, Alicia began scanning the surrounding woods, hoping that she would see a deer, or perhaps even a moose, though that could be a little terrifying being this close.

As Alicia looked into the thick of trees, something sort of tickled at the corner of her eye. Something seen, but not quite seen. Little movements that disappeared as soon as she looked their way. She kept trying to focus, looking for what she was missing, unable to see anything. It, whatever it was, always eluded her at the last minute. What was it? What was she feeling but not seeing? She felt a chill run up her spine that was not due to the quickening rain. Goosebumps broke out along her bare arms and legs. The frustration of knowing something was there, but unable to grasp it was slowly building inside of her. But she was determined. Alicia glanced back at her father, who was distracted with untying the boat while simultaneously trying to keep it from banging against the rocks along the shoreline in the increasing wind and waves. She looked back once again at the depths of the forest and this time, instead of trying to focus so intently, she let her eyes go slightly out of focus. She looked beyond and suddenly, startlingly, everything popped into clarity. She saw! Alicia stepped forward, and in.

CH. 4 A DAUGHTER LOST

Richard eventually finished the task of untying the boat. The wind had really picked up and, in the process, pulled the rope and knots tighter than he had remembered tying them. Now it was time to get home before the first few telltale drops became the promised deluge. Richard wasn't looking forward to rowing back across the lake in this wind and turned quickly to Alicia to tell her to hop on board. Except...Alicia wasn't there.

"Alicia?" There was no response.

Perhaps she had stepped behind a tree or was burrowing in a bush to grab a small snake. "Alicia, let's go!" Again, there was silence, except for the increasing rush of wind through the treetops which buoyed the sense of urgency he was feeling about getting back across the lake before the storm really hit. Glancing up, Richard saw the sky darkening; the baby blue they had rowed beneath was now a dark purply-gray. Loose pine needles were shaken free by the strengthening winds, drifting down around him, landing in his hair making his head look like a porcupine. The temperature around him had dropped by a number of degrees. He was beginning to get irritated with his daughter. How far could she have possibly gone? The last thing he wanted to do was secure the boat once again and go looking for her.

"Alicia, let's go NOW!" he called. Still there was no response.

The irritation slowly changed and now the first tinges of worry were starting to creep in. They were unwanted and unwelcome, but where could she possibly be?

Feeling a sense of unease, Richard quickly set to the task of sloppily tying the boat up once more. He then turned around and stepped toward the thick forest. "Alicia! ALICIAAA!!"

Now he was really yelling, his eyes scanning near and far for any sign of his missing daughter. Raindrops were starting to reach his face a little more frequently, running off the back of his head and down his neck. But still there was no sign of Alicia anywhere.

A lack of understanding, mixed with worry and despair, started coursing through Richard. "If this is one of your games, I am NOT amused! Come out NOW!" he called, still holding the belief that she couldn't, simply couldn't, be missing. There was nowhere to go! This small patch of sand was bordered on all sides by an almost impenetrable wall of trees and bushes. Certainly, it didn't take him that long to untie the boat, and despite there being wild animals in the forest, none of them were a threat to humans, especially in the middle of the afternoon.

"ALICIA!! ALICIA!!" Richard bellowed over and over, his calls now filled with an urgent and growing sense of panic. He tromped through the bushes never moving far from the shore, always keeping the boat in sight, just in case she really was just playing one of her favorite games. The rain had picked up quickly and his shirt was soaked, the blowing wind causing a chill to set in. Richard's mind was lost in confusion. At this moment, he had a sense of everything in the world being wrong. How could a beautiful afternoon become such a fury of nature's blessed rain and sheer terror? He spun in circles, looking, searching, calling, and yelling until his voice was hoarse. The full-blown storm could not compete with the storm raging through his head as he tried to make sense of this. Richard collapsed to the ground as the truth absorbed him, crushing him with its weight. Alicia was gone.

CH. 5 REALIZATIONS

As Alicia stepped forward she sensed, and felt, a shift in reality. A pushing through, as if encountering an extraordinarily large gust of wind that she had to use all of her energy to move past. She braced and leaned hard into the wind and, for just a moment, the hair on her arms stood up as if lifted by static electricity. As quickly as the wind stirred up, it abruptly stopped and everything was normal again. But somehow, it felt a little different.

The green of the trees was a dark almost emerald color, not like the trees she knew, which were more of a dusty grey-green. Everything looked a little brighter and the air felt warmer against her skin than it did a few minutes ago, before that crazy wind. Alicia suddenly noticed that the slapping of the lake's waves behind her had disappeared and was replaced by a sound like the gentle whisper of wind through tall grasses. She stood in awe for a moment, one hand on her hip and the other scratching her head as she tried to recognize what was around her.

"Hi!"

Alicia looked around but did not see her

dad or anyone else. Who was talking to her?

"I said, hi. You don't have to be rude and not say it back."

Alicia continued to look around, still not recognizing anything and feeling totally confused. All she saw was one golden-mantled squirrel, abundant in the area, on the old stump of a pine tree. She knew from experience that they were incredibly friendly and sociable, especially if you had nuts or some other snack to offer. Sitting in a chair outside of the cabin, you could be sure that sooner or later, a squirrel would be on your lap, poking around for a delicious treat. But for the most part, they were silent except for when they chattered at one another angrily for hogging all the food. Her furrowed brow showed the confused state of mind she found herself in. Could this voice she was hearing really be coming from that furry little thing or was she dreaming?

"Are you talking to me?" she asked half-jokingly, looking at the squirrel but expecting no answer.

"Yes, I'm talking to you," the squirrel replied. It stood up on its hind legs and stared at her, his tiny arms crossed in a scolding manner. "I've said hi twice and you so rudely did not say hi back!"

Alicia's mouth fell open so wide with surprise that you could see every one of her molars, and she found herself at a loss for words. *No, that simply cannot be!* she thought as she glanced around. Surely someone hiding behind a tree was playing a tremendous joke on her.

"That's a great way to catch flies, but not so great for talking." Alicia was sure the voice seemed to come directly from the squirrel.

"Say. Hi. Back."

"Uh... hello?" Alicia replied cautiously, deciding to play along for the moment.

"Is that a question, or a..." the tiny creature shook his head with disappointment. "Never mind. You certainly are a strange one. Allow me to introduce myself. My name is Mickey."

Again, her mouth fell open. This squirrel *was* actually speaking--to her! Was she going crazy?

"Mickey?" she asked, her confusion showing through the slow and thoughtful delivery of the familiar name. "Oh! Like Mickey Mouse?"

The squirrel's small grin turned into a small, but angry looking frown. He huffed a retort, "Do I look like a mouse to you? You know, since the barrier went up, no humans have visited here. I've heard stories passed down through generations, of how generous your kind is, especially with treats! But you are the first human child—you are a human, right? You're the first one I have ever seen here in my whole entire life. And so far, I am not impressed. Are all humans as rude as you are?"

Alicia was taken aback, not only by the fact that here she was, talking to a squirrel of all things, but that it appeared he was giving her a good scolding! "Yes, I'm a human!" she exclaimed. "And no, you don't look like a mouse. But he is the only talking rodent I've ever heard of, so you can imagine my surprise!" She relaxed her neck and shoulders, which she suddenly realized were stiff as a board. If this was really happening, and she still wasn't sure if she might be dreaming, then she supposed she would play along. "It is a pleasure to meet you, Mickey. My name is Alicia, and I do apologize for my rudeness."

"I'm gonna let that 'rodent' comment slide, because it's a beautiful day and right now I am in a good mood." The tiny creature's tail moved for the first time since their encounter, first left, then right, then up, and finally securely back down on the tree stump in a soft and re-laxed fashion. "Be warned, however. If you use that slur again," his little tail shot straight up again, "I'll not be so forgiving! Now... do you have some food?"

Alicia paused, ignoring the question, and looked around for the first time since hearing Mickey's voice. She realized that the small squirrel was right. The rain, which had been light but insistent, had completely stopped and she could see the sunlight shining bright-ly through the trees. It *was* a beautiful day! "What happened to the storm?"

"Storm? What storm? Are you daft as well

as rude?" Mickey shook his head in disbelief at the silliness being spoken by the human child. "There has been nothing but brief sprinkles of rain in the sky for a long time now, and even that gets sucked up quickly. In fact, it has become a serious problem; with the land drying up, many of us forest creatures are getting quite thirsty." Mickey smacked his lips realizing he needed a drink.

"Thirsty? But you have an entire lake filled with water right there!" Alicia said as she turned around to point at the water behind her. But to her shock and confusion, the lake was no longer there! All that remained was a vast meadow of grass, slowly turning brown under the hot sun. Oh my gosh, where was her dad?!

"Dad? DAD??"

"Who are you talking to?"

"My dad! He was right there a moment ago!" She pointed to where she had pushed through the windy portal. "Where is he? And where is the lake?" She felt a lump forming in her throat and was not going to let it get the best of her. "Where is everything?!?" Alicia asked fearfully.

"Silly girl, you left that all behind when you crossed over to the Wild Side," Mickey explained patiently.

CH. 6 THE WILD SIDE

Alicia stared in stunned silence at the meadow that, in her mind anyway, was once a beautiful blue lake. As she watched, a small bunny bounded away through the grass, startling a previously unseen flock of birds into flight. She didn't understand any of this.

Her father was just right there a moment ago. Her beloved lake, the boat, and the cabin on the other side were there and now... were they really gone? It made no sense. None at all. Maybe she really was going crazy. *What did the squirrel say about a Wild Side? What does that even mean?*

Alicia turned back toward the small squirrel, still staring at her from his perch on the log. "What is going on?" Feeling scared and confused, she crossed her arms in front of herself protectively. "What did you mean about a 'Wild Side'? Where is my family?" she asked with panic in her voice.

Mickey looked at the girl, his own confusion showing itself though his upturned lips. "You came here." He pointed a tiny finger at her then downward, finally panning the vast horizon around them in one sweeping motion.

"This is the Wild Side. How do you not know this? Nobody comes here by accident. Nobody *can* come here by accident. The Ancient Ones made sure of that."

"What Ancient Ones? What Wild Side?" Alicia flung her arms into the air with such exasperation that Mickey ducked, ever so slightly, so he would not be accidentally hit. "I don't understand what you are talking about!" Alicia shouted at the squirrel in frustration.

It dawned on Mickey that perhaps this human really didn't know about this land. It was clear to him that she was frightened. "Ok, let me start at the beginning, at least as far as I know it." He sat comfortably on his tree stump and motioned her to sit with him, but there was not enough room. Alicia felt a wave of dizziness from the confusion sweep through her head, rocking her back on her heels. Slowly she lowered herself to solid ground, nesting herself into the grass, eyes darting frantically left and right, her mind still searching for anything familiar. There was really nothing she could do but to listen to what the squirrel had to say. "The stories have been passed down through generations, from my parents, grandparents, great-grandparents, and far beyond that." Mickey paused to collect his thoughts while Alicia, fidgeting to get comfortable on the prickly grass, rested her chin on her hands. Her arms were wrapped snuggly around her legs, with hands nestled atop her raised knees. She was curled up so tightly, as if to protect herself from what she was about to hear.

"The Ancient Ones are very old beings. There is Thunderbolt on the top of the mountain, who watches over the lands and strikes with powerful lightning; Vulcan, who lives in the hot springs and provides a warm spot to gather during the long cold winters; and old Silver King, from down in the depths, ruling over the underground dwellers and hoarding the strongest magic for himself." Mickey paused for a minute in case his new friend had any questions; she remained silent and staring so he continued. "It is told that ages ago, the lands of magic and humans mingled, sharing thoughts, ideas, and resources. But the humans' desire for growth and expansion caused them to be greedy with resources. They began chopping down the trees of the forest by the hundreds, not caring about animals that called the woods home."

"That's awful!" the young girl from the *other side* interrupted.

Mickey continued, seemingly unaware of Alicia's reaction. "They diverted streams and rivers for their own use, leaving formerly lush and green regions to dry and turn brown from lack of water. They mined for precious metals, blasting away at rocks and collapsing mountains. Many animal families were forced to leave the lands their ancestors had called home. The Ancient Ones, seeing this happen to their beloved lands, came together for the first time ever, and using their combined magic, created the barrier to split the two realms and forever separate the lands of humans and magic. *Let humans destroy their own resources* was their attitude. The lands of magic would recover and continue to thrive on their own."

Alicia listened to Mickey's story with wonder and amazement and a small seed of hope grew in her chest. "So, these Ancient Ones. They have great magic, right? They could take down the barrier and let me cross back?"

"The Ancient Ones are gone," Mickey replied, dashing Alicia's hopes. "It is said that so much magic was required to build the barrier, that after it was created, they retreated to their separate homes to try and recover their lost energy. They have not been seen since."

With this disappointment came an understanding of her situation, and tears finally flooded her eyes. "So, I'm stuck here?" Alicia wailed, hiding her face in the gap between her knees and chest, heaving great sobs.

"But you must have incredible magic yourself!" Mickey insisted. "You came through the barrier. You crossed over. Only the most powerful could do such a thing."

"But ... I didn't ... didn't mean to..." Alicia could barely speak through the tears, her body shaking from their force. "I didn't use any power or magic. I just stepped forward!"

"Then just step back," Mickey said.

"I CAN'T! I DON'T KNOW HOW!" she screamed, slamming her small fists on the ground, wanting to punch something to release her sorrow and frustration.

Mickey, not knowing how to respond, simply watched.

Alicia sat there, her sobs diminishing, while Mickey by her side waited patiently.

"What am I going to do?" she asked, hiccupping with the last of her tears. "My mom, my dad, everything I know and love, is gone?"

"Well, not everything. I'm still here."

"Yes, but you're a squirrel! How can you help me?!?"

"There you go being impolite again." Mickey stood ready to walk away but turned and looked up at his new friend who was still sitting in her spot on the ground. "I understand this is all a shock right now, so I'll continue to forgive your behavior." He looked up at her with stern, focused eyes. "But you are lucky that I found you." He paused, his expression softening as he thought for a moment. "I am going to be your guide here in the Wild Side! At least until you learn your way around. I know where all the best berries are."

"I know those too!" Alicia exclaimed. "I know all about huckleberries."

"Oh yeah? You think you're so smart." Mickey was relieved to be having a normal conversation. "Do you know where the best burrows are to stay warm at night?"

"Burrows?" Alicia cocked her head sideways feeling slightly confused, and looked at Mickey. "What would I know about burrows?" she said, sadness returning to her voice. "The best way to stay warm is snuggled between my parents on the couch in front of the fire, with a warm comforter draped over our legs. Or in my warmest winter coat when my friends and I are outside." Tears began to form in her eyes again. "That was the exact plan for tonight. My mom was going to read to me in front of the fire." A small sob escaped her throat.

Mickey paused in his questioning, noticing again how hard this must be on the girl. "Alicia, please don't worry. I really can help you," he said with concern in his voice, his small fuzzy features softening. "Burrows can be very nice and warm, and I'll snuggle with you since you don't have a warm winter coat or a fire or a cabin. I'll help you search for what remaining water there is so you can drink. And most important of all, I'll help you avoid the eyes of Bristleback."

Alicia wiped the tears away with the back of her hand. "What's a Bristleback?" She stood up from the warm spot she had created sitting in the grass ready to trust and follow Mickey.

"Ha, see? You don't know everything," he responded, allowing a little bit of the mockery to return to his voice, but only a little. "That is why I am going to keep you company and be your guide," Mickey said, some of his delight and belligerence returning as well. "Listen, I understand you miss your family, I really do. I haven't seen my family in ages, either. I think I have brothers and sisters that I have never even met! But I'm here with you and I promise to teach you all that I can." Mickey hopped up onto a low branch on a nearby tree to make sure Alicia could hear him. "In return, you can let me ride on your shoulder and help keep the nasty foxes away. They're always yapping and fussing and trying to dig in your home and eat you. Never a moment's rest with those nasty things around. Oh, and the jaybirds with their constant screeching. You just find a pine nut and they come swooping down to steal it! Go find your own food, you camp robbers! Speaking of food," he pointed at Alicia, "you can help find that too!"

Alicia dried her tears and looked at Mickey. She didn't know what to make of this creature. She was used to feeding squirrels peanuts out of her hand and watching them caper around the front yard of the cabin. And now, here was one standing in front of her, talking to her. Actually talking! Was she going crazy? She felt so lost and alone. How could this person--not even a person, just a small animal--help her survive? Sure, her dad had taught her much over the past few years, but she was still young. She was terrified and an-guished over the disappearance of everything she'd known. Her dad was gone. Her mom was gone. Her friends must be gone, too. The way she felt right now, it might as well be the whole world that was gone! Could she really trust in this one tiny creature and the hope for companionship that he offered?

She didn't know, but it seemed at the mo-ment her options were limited and her mind was foggy. She was strong and had spent hours upon hours by herself in these woods. Perhaps the squirrel was right. She was willing to learn more, and maybe with his help, she could find her way back to the world she knew. It would be good to have a friend right now. She set her jaw and made a decision.

"Okay, Mickey. It's a deal." She reached out and the squirrel hopped into her hand, scampering up her arm and onto her shoulder.

"This is going to be grand," he pronounced. "Now about that food. Let's head east. I'm hungry and I know where there's a good patch of berry bushes."

Alicia was too. She and her father had not brought any food with them to the beach. So, if the squirrel was suggesting there was food to the east, then east it was. She searched for a strong stick, just a little longer than waist height, and found an old fallen branch that looked sturdy. It was always a good idea to have a walking stick when setting out on an adventure.

CH. 7 THE DRYING

They walked for an hour, all the while Mickey chattered away on her shoulder about this thing or that. The scent of fresh pine trees was in the air, reminding her of the family room at home during Christmas season. As they walked, the unmistakable buzz of small mosquitos filled her ears, causing Alicia to swing her arms wildly to chase them away.

Mickey dodged her swats at the irritating bugs and chattered non-stop, describing all the bushes, plants, and mushrooms, even though Alicia knew quite a few of them already. She was fascinated by the little furry creature sitting on her shoulder, so happily blabbering on and on, and politely let him continue uninterrupted. After all, there was still so much knowledge to be gained, she thought. Douglas firs and lodgepole pines covered the hills, while in the open spaces they could see the beautiful red and orange colors of Indian paintbrush, or the purples of lupine and lavender. The forest was full of so much variety, if you took the time to look.

"Those are morels," Mickey said excitedly. "They are a special kind of mushroom that is usually difficult to find. But after a forest fire, oh my gosh, they grow like crazy! Delicious!" And one second later he tapped Alicia's cheek and pointed, "You see that one with the red marks on the stem? That's nature's way of saying 'Stay away.'"

Other times he would draw her attention to the sounds in the woods. "Do you hear that?" They stopped moving and focused on a hissing sound peppered with occasional plops, which Alicia imagined were tiny pebbles cascading into a pile. "There is a stream nearby. Look for a group of thick, green vegetation, or a swarm of dragonflies." Sure enough, Alicia found a trickle of water cool and clean, near banks that were lined with moss. She could drink from it by cupping her hands and scooping up the delicious liquid.

At last they found a wonderfully big patch

of huckleberries, ripe and plump. Alicia began picking and popping them into her mouth as fast as she could, savoring the delicious sweetness with just a hint of bitter from the skins. The fat, purple berries stained her fingers, lips, and tongue. Alicia smiled at Mickey, feeling the first hint of happiness since leaving the beach and what she was quickly growing to think of as "her world."

After gorging on berries, Alicia and Mickey rested on a pile of soft pine needles. For the first time, she really took in her surroundings and noticed how brown much of the landscape was. How odd, especially in July. The snows should have melted from the higher mountaintops and flowed down to moisten the soil, creating all sorts of green growth. Then she remembered what Mickey had told her.

"You said the land was drying up. What

did you mean?"

"Just what I said," Mickey replied. "The water is getting taken and there is no longer any left for the smaller plants or us forest creatures. We call it The Drying."

"The Drying?" the young botany enthusiast searched her mind for the term but could not find it. "But where is the water going? The land should be filled with the runoff from the snow melt."

"It's because of old Gran'Tree."

"Who's that?" Alicia asked.

"Gran'Tree is the tallest, widest, most ginormous tree in the whole forest!" Mickey exclaimed stretching himself as much as he could to demonstrate the massiveness of this tree. "He is so tall; his top almost touches the clouds and his branches stretch out farther than Bristleback's arms. He reaches out so wide he blocks the sun, and nothing can grow underneath him, so he stands alone in a huge, dusty, barren clearing. His giant roots reach far underground and he sucks up every bit of water, keeping it all to himself. I don't know how much longer this forest can survive."

"Hasn't anybody spoken with him? Surely, he must see what is happening."

"We are all too small," Mickey explained. "We try to speak, but he is so tall, he cannot hear when we call up to him. Or if he does, he just ignores it. We don't know what to do. Many of the creatures are planning to make the long journey south in search of better lands. But this is my home and I can't just leave."

Alicia understood, once again, feeling the loss of her own home intensely. She forced those thoughts out of her head and stood up.

"I guess we should be on our way. You

mentioned knowing of burrows to sleep in. It's getting dark and I don't want to spend the night under the stars."

"Oh yes, oh yes, I know all the best burrows! So warm and cozy. Let's go!"

They set off again, heading east, toward what? Alicia could not say.

She only hoped that she would discover some clue to finding her way home again.

CH. 8 TASTY TREATS

That evening, Alicia and Mickey spent the night in a hole in the ground. It was actually quite spacious though not exactly "warm and cozy" like Mickey had described, and Alicia was thankful for the towel she still had with her from the beach. It was large and wrapped her like a blanket, keeping the chill of the evening away. Mickey found a perfect spot by her arm in which to curl up, and together, they closed their eyes.

"Goodnight, Mickey," Alicia whispered in the dark. "I'm glad you were there when I came through. I don't know what I would have done today without you there to explain things to me. So thank you."

"You are very welcome," Mickey replied. "I am glad I met you too. This is all so very interesting. I never imagined I would meet a *human*. Sweet dreams, Alicia. Try not to roll over on me during the night."

Alicia smiled briefly at this, then fell asleep quickly and was lost in dreams of her family and her bed in the cabin with its large downy comforter.

She awoke in the morning with a start, confused at first, but slowly remembering the events of the previous day. Remembering where she was and who she was with. Mickey had yet to stir, so she gently lifted her arm from around him and moved away, trying not to disturb his slumber, and crawled out of the hole into the crisp morning air. She didn't mind the cold and anyway--she knew the day would warm soon enough.

"Good morning, Lish."

Alicia spun toward the hole she had crawled out of moments before, her eyes became brighter as her mouth formed a wide grin, then she saw Mickey emerging. Her features quickly turned into a scowl when she realized who was speaking. "Don't ever call me that. Only my father can call me that," she said, a note of sourness in her voice.

"Fine, okay, don't get huffy, A-li-ci-a," he said, slowly drawing out her name with exaggeration.

"Thank you, very much." Alicia looked off into the distance, thoughtfully. "You know, I think I want to see this Gran'Tree. Maybe I could talk to him. Maybe I can make him understand."

"Sure, I can take you there," Mickey said. "And you can talk your silly head off. He won't listen. He never listens."

"Yes, but you said I was the first human child you had seen here. Maybe this Gran'Tree will be surprised as well. That shock will force him to pay attention to me."

"You can believe that, sure," Mickey said, unconvinced. "It will take several days, and really, what else were we planning to do?" He stopped talking and looked up at Alicia. Something she said had changed his mind. "So, okay, let's go see Gran'Tree. But first... breakfast!"

Alicia gathered up her towel, Mickey climbed onto her shoulder, and with his guidance, they headed south to find the source of these problems.

Before long, Alicia found a trail through the woods, carved into the soil by centuries of deer and more ancient creatures that lived in this realm. Alicia imagined that once upon a time this was a road for gnomes and trolls and other assorted fae folk who once called this land home. Do they still live here? That she didn't know, but the possibility of seeing one kept her eyes flicking this way and that.

After spending the previous day slogging through bushes and stepping over fallen logs, walking down the relatively clear trail made the going much easier and faster. The day flowed by, and the two of them fell into a routine of walking and resting, with small detours to find fresh water, stopping to eat berries and even the occasional pine nuts when they could find them.

They spent the next night in a different burrow, the hard-packed dirt around them acting like insulation against the cold of the evening. In the dark, Alicia's thoughts once again went to her family, and this time, she couldn't contain it. Tears bubbled up and she cried herself to sleep with Mickey curled tight against her, sensing her sadness and trying to offer what comfort he could. Eventually, she quieted down and her even breathing signaled to her companion that she was asleep. Mickey settled in as well and quickly lost himself in squirrel dreams filled with nuts and dust baths.

The morning brought a new day and with it, a new determination.

Alicia awoke, shook off sleep, wiped crust from the corners of her eyes, and set her mind to the goal at hand. She was convinced that if she just spoke with the great tree, she could make him see what he was doing to the forest. And maybe, just maybe, he could help her find a way back to her parents and her world.

The day progressed with the same uneventfulness of the previous day, with long stretches of hiking interrupted by stops for water and huckleberries. Alicia was thankful for the strong walking stick she had found, as it helped with the uphill sections of the forest path.

"With all these berries and nuts I've been eating, I'm starting to feel like a bear!" Alicia exclaimed, beating her chest like some strange cross between a cartoon bear and a gorilla, feeling a wild energy inside of her.

"You're starting to look like one too," said Mickey, smiling back at her. "The next stream we find, I am definitely making you wash your face! It's covered in dirt!"

Alicia stuck her tongue out at the squirrel, making a horrible visage that her parents would find almost unrecognizable.

"What is this, then?" Alicia spun toward

the new voice. "It looks like a human child, and a lovely, tasty rodent."

Standing several feet away, a small fox was looking at her. Mickey saw what she was staring at and immediately ran up her leg, all the way to her shoulder, and wriggled behind her neck, peering intently at the fox from underneath Alicia's hair.

The fox was about the size of a small dog, maybe a Yorkshire terrier or a beagle. Its fur was straight and golden, except for a small patch of grey around the muzzle. It had a large bushy tail. Alicia noticed some old scars along its flank where no fur grew, as if a sharp claw had raked down its side. She backed away a step, unsure of this newcomer.

"Tasty and delicious," came a similar voice from behind. Alicia spun to see a second fox who was almost identical to the first except, perhaps, with more youthful features and none of the grey. This newcomer snuck up behind her and she felt a chill of terror run up her spine. She was trapped with a hungry, sharp-toothed predator on either side of her.

"And he looks chubby and plump enough for us all to share!" said a third fox. She saw that a fourth had appeared as well. The girl was surrounded. She felt Mickey quaking like a leaf against her neck, and her hands were sweaty now.

"Alicia," Mickey whispered with a trembling voice. "Protect me, pleeeeease."

Alicia was terrified by this new situation and felt a bead of sweat trickle down her neck. She knew the woods could be dangerous, but things had been going so well she hadn't given it much thought. Now a new fear gripped her; she had a knot in the pit of her stomach and had to remind herself to breathe. Alicia was frozen in place but worked hard to strengthen her resolve; after all, her tiny new friend was counting on her size and human-ness to save them. She dug deep to find confidence, even though she could see the small sharp fangs and claws of the foxes, which terrified her.

"Don't worry, Mickey. I won't let them have you." Alicia said with more courage than she felt. She raised the walking stick she was carrying, holding it out like a sword, ready to give the first fox that made a move a good whack on the nose. She had fallen off her bicycle more than once in her young life, she thought to herself, so she knew how much a blow to the nose could hurt!

"What are you going to do with that twig?" the first and eldest-looking fox, most likely the leader, snarled with disdain. "You see these scars? I've faced down stronger creatures than you." He looked Alicia up and down, growling quietly to expose his sharp teeth, enjoying her fear. "Compared to a mountain lion, you are nothing," he said in a menacing voice.

"Come on, just give him to us," one of his companions yipped. "This will be so much simpler for you in the long run. No fuss, no muss. Well, not much muss, anyway. We intend to eat every part."

The other foxes barked and yapped with canine laughter at the sick joke. Slowly they began to walk in a counter-clockwise motion, circling Alicia, trying to confuse and intimidate her with this distraction.

"Hold still, stop walking!" she yelled at them. But still they continued to circle, slowly, slowly, 'round, and 'round. Alicia had to keep spinning her head one way or the other to keep them all in sight. She started to feel dizzy, but knew she had to stay strong.

Unexpectedly, the leader barked sharply, drawing the young girl's attention. Alicia spun in his direction but knew immediately that she had made a mistake. The fox directly behind her lunged and she felt its sharp, filthy claws dig into the back of her bare leg drawing lines of blood as he attempted to run up her body and launch himself at the squirrel hidden away underneath her hair. Mickey clung to her shirt for dear life, as Alicia screamed in pain and twirled the other way, swinging her stick as hard as she could. But the fox, missing the small squirrel on this attempt, had quickly fallen away and rejoined the rest in the circle. The evil band of foxes slowly slinked around and around the poor, frightened girl who was now bleeding. Alicia winced, feeling the sting from the large scratches along her leg.

The fox who had attacked her licked Alicia's blood from his claws, exaggeratingly savoring the taste with his long tongue. Blood coated his teeth and lips as he drew them back with an evil canine smile.

"If you just give it to us, this will all be over," the leader spoke calmly, but with an underlying threat in his tone of voice. "You can go about your way, whichever way that may be, and we'll go ours. You are a human, right? What is that one fat little squirrel to a human?"

Hearing his words, Alicia felt all the anger and frustration of the past couple days boil to the surface. The getting lost, sleeping in the dirt, eating nothing but berries and nuts, losing her father, losing her WHOLE LIFE! Who has been by her side this whole time? Helping and guiding her? Mickey, that's who!

"What is one little squirrel, you ask?" she snarled angrily at the fox showing *him* all of *her* big white teeth, raising and shaking her stick for emphasis. "He's family!! He is the only family I have now, you hear me! And you! Can't! Have! Him!"

She lunged rapidly toward the lead fox, swinging her stick with both hands this time. The fox was taken by surprise with this sudden attack and Alicia hit him hard, right smack in the side of his rib cage. The fox yelped as it tried to scramble away. Alicia spun to attack the next one as Mickey clung desperately to her shirt. Not watching where she was stepping, her sandal caught on an upturned root, and down she went, landing hard on her rear end.

Slow, cruel laughter rose up from the

foxes. "Is that all you've got?" the eldest asked with nothing but contempt for the girl. She had gotten one hit on him and he wasn't planning to let that go unpunished.

"Her blood is exquisite," whispered the fox who had scratched her. "I think we could feed on this one for quite some time."

Cautiously, the pack began to move closer. She could see drool forming at the corners of their lips, where they pulled back to bare sharp fangs. She fearfully realized that once they were done with Mickey, they would come for her too.

Alicia held the walking stick, her only source of protection, out in front of her. She could feel blood running down the back of her leg from the scratches left by the attacking fox. Her bottom was sore from where she just landed on it, and she was oh so tired.

For a second time, tears filled her eyes and blurred her vision. As the foxes continued to slowly creep closer, they took their time because they knew she was outnumbered.

They wanted to savor this victory over a human. Alicia was exhausted, hurting inside and out, and did not know if she had any fight left in her.

"I'm looking forward to this," the eldest of the pack whispered fiercely and with anticipation. "You are going to be delicious."

Suddenly, quick as a flash, something black zoomed out of nowhere and slammed into one of the foxes, drawing a sharp squeal of pain from him. It was gone as fast as it appeared. The foxes were so startled, they stopped slinking toward the girl and began looking up, down, left, and right. Again, almost faster than the eye could see, the black thing swooped down, hitting another fox in the side, sending him yelping to the ground. Alicia didn't know what this black thing could be, but she felt strength flowing back into her limbs thanks to this mysterious attacker. Could it be their savior?

A third time, the black thing came flying in, but this time Alicia went on the attack too. Between the two of them, they whacked and pummeled the final pair of foxes still trying to attack, breaking the menace of the moment.

"Come brothers, it's not worth it," the leader yipped. Together, the pack crawled to their feet and quickly ran off, their hunger forgotten for the time being.

"*CAW! CAW*! That was *CAW*-some!" The black thing came and landed on a branch above Alicia's head and now she could see that what she had mistaken for solid black was actually a beautiful blend of black and dark blue feathers.

Mickey crawled out from under Alicia's hair and onto her shoulder. "That's a Steller's jay!" he pronounced. "They'll steal your food if you're not careful."

"Pleased to *CAW* make your acquaintance," the jay screeched. "My name is Briar!" Alicia looked at the bird and was taken by how handsome he was. His wings and feathers were a rich, royal dark blue, while his head and shoulders were a deep shade of black. A small crown of feathers poked up from the top of his head like a mohawk. The bird looked at them with his dark round eyes.

"Briar?" Alicia asked.

"*CAW*! Yes! My beak is as sharp as a briar *CAW* patch. You saw what I did to those *CAW* foxes, right?" the bird screeched, proudly.

"I did! Thank you so very, very much!" replied Alicia. "You saved our lives! But why did you rescue us?"

"I heard *CAW* what you said to those foxes about family *CAW*! I too am without family," Briar said, wistfully. "My cousins, the *CAW* camp robbers, always travel in threes. But me, I *CAW* am always alone."

"Oh, that is so sad," Alicia said with regret in her voice. "But you don't have to be alone. You can travel with us. We have a long road ahead of us and we would very much welcome your company."

"Says you," spoke up Mickey, his natural distrust of the jay giving his voice a note of anger. "Didn't you hear me say they steal your food if you're not careful? They are natural-born thieves!"

For all that a bird can show emotion, Briar

actually looked hurt. "*CAW* Oh, I would never do that! Not to my *CAW* friends anyway. You have my word," he promised.

"What good is the word of a thief?" Mickey responded. To Alicia, it was clear that Mickey had previous run-ins with the jays of the forest and was none too quick to forgive. She wanted to stop this argument before it got out of control.

"I think we can trust him, Mickey," Alicia said, reassuringly. "After all, he did just save our lives. And again, thank you so much for that, Mr. Briar."

"No, no, *CAW* please. Just call me Briar. And you are very welcome." The jay continued, "I never liked those foxes anyway. Always *CAW* yapping and making trouble, even in the middle of the night. It's impossible to get a *CAW* good night's sleep with them around. I have to fly to the very tops of the *CAW* tallest trees to escape their noise."

"Okay, I will call you Briar," Alicia said. "And this is my great friend and traveling companion, Mickey. We are traveling to see Gran'Tree. I am going to speak with him and ask him if he will stop drinking all the water. We need to stop The Drying." *And maybe help me find a way home*, but she didn't say that out loud for fear of jinxing it.

"Pleased to meet you... I guess," Mickey said with caution in his voice, clearly unhappy with this new situation. "But just so you know, I'm going to be keeping a very close eye on you."

"That sounds like a *CAW*-some adventure. I would be most pleased to a-*CAW*-mpany you on your journey!" Briar screeched with joy. "I've never seen Gran'Tree myself, only heard tales. I am sure he is a *CAW*-razy sight to behold. And I know about The Drying. I've *CAW* seen it and it's a terrible thing!"

And so they set out, the twosome now a threesome. How much further they would have to travel, Alicia didn't know. But she knew one thing. Even if it wasn't Mom and Dad, or anyone she knew well, with these two new friends, she could have a chance at having a family again.

CH. 9 A SURPRISING CONVERSATION

The next couple days passed without incident. Briar would fly ahead, scanning the landscape from above and search for the best, most direct paths. From his vantage, he was able to spot the glint of water far more easily than Alicia or Mickey could from the ground. True to his word, whenever they found a patch of berries or a fallen pine cone filled with nuts, Briar would only eat his share and never, ever, ever attempt to steal food from the others. *At least not when they were looking*, Mickey thought. The squirrel was not yet completely trusting of the bird, and would have sworn, if asked, that he saw the same mistrust pass through Briar's head more than once.

Briar was unsure about spending time underground, choosing instead to remain in the branches above while he slept. He would keep Alicia and Mickey company in the evenings, tucked away in the dark confines for warmth, chatting before returning to the branches for the night. One night, as the three of them were settling down into another burrow for their evening conversation, there came a soft rumbling from the earth beneath them.

Alicia quickly looked about to see if she could figure out the source, but there was very little light in the den to begin with, and with darkness quickly approaching, she could not see much of anything.

"What is that?" she asked as the intensity of the rumbling grew stronger.

"That, sweet one, is Bristleback," said Mickey. "He must be nearby."

"Bristleback?"

"*CAW*," Briar called as he took up the story. "Bristleback is the last remaining *CAW* mountain troll. Big as a hill, maybe two! He searches far *CAW* and wide for more of his *CAW*-ind. But sadly, there are none left."

"Most left long ago," Mickey continued, "never to return. The few that remained slowly dried up because of the lack of water and turned into boulders. Now Bristleback is all that is left and even he is fading, though he is still very dangerous. If you see Bristleback, you need to hope with all your heart that he doesn't see you."

"His *CAW* mouth is filled with teeth like rocks! They are perfect for *CAW* grinding up bones. His back is *CAW*-overed with long stiff hair, like the burnt remains of trees after a forest fire. And he carries a large club for *CAW*-lobbering his prey on the head to knock them out before gobbling them up!"

Mickey nodded vigorously, listening to Briar describe the monster. "It would be best if we did all we could to avoid him. Bristleback is danger with a capital D!"

The rumble slowly faded, and Alicia guessed that the fearsome Bristleback must be moving away. She fell asleep that night, remembering the mountains around the lake that looked like slumbering giants and wondered if they were related in any way to the mountain troll.

The next day, as they were taking a break from endless walking to drink from a quiet stream, a movement on the far side grabbed their attention. Fearing the foxes had sneakily returned, Alicia backed slowly away from the stream, picked up her walking stick, and prepared for an attack. The bushes parted and a large head with pointy ears and the softest eyes she had ever seen poked through. One of the forest deer emerged, cautiously watching Alicia for a moment, as deer always do, before bending her head to drink from the stream.

"Oh my gosh, you are beautiful," Alicia exclaimed quietly, turning to face the deer. "My name is Alicia, and these are my friends,

Mickey and Briar."

"Deer do not talk," Mickey explained. "It's not that they are dumb, quite the opposite as a matter of fact. They just prefer the silence of the woods and honor it with silence of their own."

"Hello, young one," the voice came from nowhere, but it was everywhere at the same time.

Alicia tensed in surprise, startled at the beautiful, eerie sound that appeared in her mind. An image resolved itself in her head–a view of high mountains covered in wildflowers--Alicia felt a sudden cool chill across her skin. She stared into the deer's eyes and saw a spark deep inside. She knew this thought was coming from the deer, but how did she know this?

"Yes, I can understand your language,

and I can speak to you as well. Not out loud, but silently, from within. My understanding of your language is limited, but I can send you images as well. Places I have seen and lived."

"She is speaking to me, in my mind," Alicia said with breathless wonder.

"My name is Fiona and I come from the highlands to the south."

"She says her name is Fiona," Alicia explained to Mickey and Briar. That must have been an image of Fiona's homeland she saw a moment ago.

Alicia focused her mind and imagined herself saying, "I am very pleased to meet you, Fiona." The deer must have heard because Alicia understood a serene response.

"Likewise. What brings a human child to this side? I have never seen your kind before, though my herd told stories."

"What do you mean, her name is Fiona?" Mickey interjected, looking confused. "Speaking to you in your mind? I hear nothing of the sort! Have you lost your marbles? All I see is you staring at that deer."

"I *CAW*-not hear anything either," Briar screeched. "I don't understand this magic. As long as I have lived, I have never heard of a talking deer."

"Quiet, guys, give me a moment. I need to speak with Fiona. And for the record, before I showed up here, I had never heard of a talking squirrel, and the only birds I heard talk were parrots. And they weren't actually talking, just mimicking sounds. So, shush!"

"Speak with Fiona?" Mickey looked at her curiously.

Alicia then told the deer her whole story, including the afternoon spent swimming at the beach with her father, the foxes and their scary attack, and how she met both of her newfound friends. She worked very hard to "think" images back to Fiona. She focused her mind on her beloved cabin, her mom and dad, and so many other things. Fiona watched her intently the entire time, listening closely to the incredible tale without interrupting the human child. Mickey and Briar waited nearby, grumbling to themselves about time wasted, their hunger and the need to find food, and rude humans.

"Shush she says," Mickey paced back and forth, kicking a small rock. "She told me to shush! Why should I shush? She's not even talking!"

"And now, we are on our way to see Gran'Tree. The journey has been much harder and longer than I expected. I confess my legs are tired and my feet are sore."

"I have traveled from the lands of Gran'Tree. I have seen The Drying spreading. I am sorry to tell you that you still have quite far to go," Fiona responded. She looked at the girl, examining her with big brown eyes. "It is against my nature to associate with those outside of my kind. In my experience, that always leads to danger." An image of wolves flashed into the girl's mind and she flinched in fright. "But I am moved by your story, young one. I have also seen the destruction The Drying is causing. If I can help, I would be happy to do so. I am not that strong, but you are small, and I believe I could carry you, at least for a little while."

"That would be wonderful and amazing," Alicia thought to the deer in return. She could not wait to share the news with Mickey and Briar. She turned to her friends and spoke faster than ever, explaining to them once again that she could speak with the deer using just her thoughts. Mickey and Briar both took the news with amazement, having never spoken with deer before. They had no reason to doubt this new friend, so why not believe it's possible? They never even considered trying to speak to a deer before. Strangely enough, however, they weren't able to see thoughts and hear words from Fiona. So they had to rely on Alicia as their translator. While they weren't affected like Alicia was with all the traveling, what with Mickey riding on her shoulder and Briar riding the high winds, they could see the toll that travel had taken on their human companion and felt a strong concern for her. Both of them thanked Fiona kindly for her graciousness, through Alicia of course, and welcomed her as a new member of their troupe. This band of merry travelers was beginning to understand that, despite their great differences, they shared similar feelings about needing companionship. The truth was, they were bound together by a common goal: getting Gran'Tree to listen.

Fiona bent her front knees, lowering herself closer to the ground so Alicia could climb on her back. The excited girl approached, reaching out to delicately touch the deer. The hair on Fiona's back was short, coarse, and rubbed rough against Alicia's legs as she gently climbed on. When she was seated firmly, Fiona rose and started walking back in the direction she had come from. Mickey, once again on his perch on top of Alicia's shoulder, whispered into the girl's ear, "Well, this is definitely a first."

"For all of us," Alicia replied. "For all of us."

CH. 10 TRAVELING COMPANIONS

As the group proceeded down the ancient trail, one problem was immediately made apparent. Fiona's hair was just too short to hang on to, and with no mane to grab, anytime they moved faster than a walk, Alicia would immediately start slipping from one side to another. Trying to keep her balance on Fiona's small frame was an impossible task and there were hills to climb ahead. She needed to figure out something to help her stay put so Fiona could move freely.

"Wait, wait," Alicia exclaimed. "I think we need to figure out a solution here. I'm slipping too much! This just won't work at any speed faster than we were already going."

"You could gather twigs and *CAW* pine needles and build a nest on her back!" Briar offered helpfully.

Mickey stared at the bird, incredulously. "That is ridiculous! Humans don't ride in nests!" He looked at Alicia. "You don't ride in nests, do you?"

"Haha, of course not!" Alicia laughed. "Thank you for the suggestion, Briar, but no, we will need to come up with another solution.

If only we had some rope."

Alicia looked around but didn't see anything lying on the ground that could be used.

"What about that?" Mickey asked.

Alicia looked up toward where he was pointing and saw long strands of black moss hanging from the tree branches.

"That's called witch's hair," Mickey eagerly explained. "The legend goes that on some nights, when the sky is clear and the moon is full, witches go flying through the woods. They have to dodge trees here and there, and their long black hair gets caught in the branches. Maybe we could use that!"

"I have many cousins that know *CAW* how to weave and I have learned a thing or two from watching them. I can *CAW* help," Briar said.

"And I can climb up in the high tree

branches and chew some free!" said Mickey, not wanting to be left out.

"That sounds like a wonderful idea," said Alicia, smiling at her helpful friends. "Fiona, would it be ok with you if I tied something around your neck to hang onto?" She closed her eyes and sent a mental image to Fiona, imagining what this yet-to-be-woven thing would look like.

"As long as it's not too tight," Fiona thought back. "If it helps us get to Gran'Tree faster and end The Drying, I can tolerate it."

"Great," Alicia said, conveying to the rest of the group Fiona's response. "Let's get started."

Together, the three of them worked to design the contraption, with Mickey climbing up and down in the tree branches, each time bringing back another mouthful of witch's hair, its long length trailing behind him as he moved. Briar quickly showed Alicia what he had learned from the other birds and they both worked on weaving the strands into a long, strong continuous piece. Alicia looked around at her small group and it filled her heart with warmth to see everyone putting aside their differences and working as a team to solve this problem. It took quite a bit of the witch's hair, and quite a bit of time, but in the end they created a loop that was strong and fit snugly around Fiona's neck, without being too tight, of course.

Alicia climbed once again onto Fiona's back and grabbed hold of the woven strap. Remembering the scratchiness of her friend's hair, Alicia jumped back off and draped her towel, which she usually wore tied around her waist, around Fiona's middle. It was not quite big enough to tie the ends together, so Mickey scampered back up the tree for more witch's hair so that another shorter length of rope could be woven to secure the blanket on Fiona's back. When that was done Alicia climbed aboard, wiggled her bottom to make sure she and the towel were secure and proclaimed, "I think I can manage much better with this. Thank you everyone for your help." She sent Fiona a silent question and said aloud to her friends, "Is everybody ready?"

A chorus of "yes" filled the air as Fiona looked around and gave Alicia a knowing glance of approval. With that, the group headed out, toward what end she didn't know, but this time of bonding and problem solving made her hopeful for the future.

They made good progress now that Alicia felt more secure, thanks to the neck strap on

Fiona. Once she found her balance and settled in, able to hang on with one hand while still carrying her walking stick in the other, Alicia gave the go-ahead and Fiona was able to pick up her pace a bit. The trails flew by underneath them. Alicia almost felt like Briar, flying through the woods with the wind blowing her hair out behind her. She was a natural athlete, so riding Fiona was surprisingly easy.

Alicia could see snakes and other small creatures scurrying out of Fiona's way. Briar kept pace with them above, taking pleasure in spending time with his unlikely companions. Mickey too felt the sense of speed that he had never experienced before, riding on the girl's shoulder, holding securely to a lock of hair, and feeling the wind in his face. It was all a wonderful sensation.

Alicia was in such good spirits that she

started singing some of the songs she had learned from her father. Songs sung at family barbeques or around campfires in the evenings as her father softly strummed the guitar. Briar tried to join her in song, but despite being a bird, his singing voice was more of a screech that quickly had the others politely asking him to simply listen.

The next few days were spent riding, harvesting berries, and stopping for small drinks of water whenever it was available. They were all getting tired and thirsty from the long trip but kept up light conversation so their mood wouldn't turn sour. Mickey told Alicia more stories about what it was like to be a squirrel and harvest food to store up for the cold winter months when he would sleep for long stretches at a time. He talked about venturing out at night, always careful to watch the shadows for the telltale signs of an owl gliding silent as a feather above. Alicia knew rodents were part of the owl's food chain and was happy this little guy, her new best friend Mickey, was so smart.

Briar taught her the ways of the birds, including which bugs were the best and which you should leave alone because they released a most awful taste in your mouth when you picked them up. Alicia was positive that ALL bugs released an awful taste. He also described what it was like to simply open your wings and feel currents of air pass beneath, knowing exactly which way to tilt and turn to follow them to your destination.

Fiona told her all about the highlands, and how exhilarating it was to bound through a meadow, stirring up pollen and the scents of flowers around you as you raced through. She talked about how bright the colors appeared to her huge, liquid eyes, and how clear the sounds were to her huge, pointy ears. These words were accompanied by an onslaught of images that were dazzling and almost too confusing for Alicia, but she took it all in with wonder, seeing the world through the deer's eyes. She had never been so intimately attached to an animal before, so this experience–actually seeing the world through Fiona's eyes–was unexpected and incredible.

The others could not hear Fiona's words, nor it seemed could Fiona understand Mickey or Briar. So, Alicia became the translator for the group and thus reinforced everything she was learning through repetition. Alicia acquired even more knowledge about the woods than she had ever imagined possible, and in turn, told stories about her own world. The animals were fascinated to hear about roads of solid stone and machines that had no mouths to sing with and yet created beautiful music.

They asked her to tell them again about the giant birds of metal that weren't actually birds but flew through the skies anyway. That story confused Briar more than he had ever been in his life. How could anything fly with wings that do not flap? He tried spreading his wings to test the breezes on a windy day, but none were strong enough to lift him up to the currents where he could simply soar. Alicia could not explain why that was, or how her flying machines could get into the sky without flapping the wings she had described. Fiona and Mickey had to admit they were confused, as well.

Though her stories left her friends befuddled, learning so much about the forest transported Alicia to thoughts of her previous life and telling her dad about what she wanted to be when she grew up. The memories brought with them her feelings of uncertainty. How long had it been? A week now? More? She was losing her sense of time, being out here in the forest. With everything she was learning, Alicia would have made an amazing botanist. But that dream was gone now, wasn't it?

Did they even have jobs on the Wild Side? Would she ever even see another human being, or like Mowgli in one of her favorite stories that mother would read to her, was she doomed to live out her life in the company of wild beasts? At least Mowgli eventually escaped the jungle and returned to the ways of man. Would she discover a way back as well? The more time passed, the less likely that looked.

On this particular day, she was pulled from her thoughts by the sudden awareness of the landscape changing. They were entering an area barren of trees. Clearly a fire had swept through this mountainside, probably caused by one of the many lightning strikes that occurred during the stormy season. It must have happened recently, because as of yet, there was no new growth coming from the seeds buried in the soil which awaited the fire to crack their shells and allow them to sprout. All that remained were a few charred trunks, pointing to the sky like... like...

The words of Briar came flooding back to her. "Long stiff hair, like the burnt remains of trees after a forest fire."

Oh, NO!

"Fiona, Fiona, we need to get out of here immediately!" Alicia thought with urgency.

"Why, what's wrong?"

"What's wrong? I think we might be on the back of--"

Suddenly, the entire world around them shook. With a tremendous growl, the earth started lifting. Fiona and Alicia along with Mickey began a slow slide down the side of the hill they were on, which was quickly becoming much steeper. With a screech, Briar took flight. From his vantage point, he could see what was happening and he became so frightened that his wings froze for a moment and he began to lose elevation.

"*CAW CAW* OH NO, OH NO!"

They had found Bristleback. And even worse. Much, much worse.

Bristleback had found them.

CH. II THE LAST MOUNTAIN

Their slide down the mountain continued to accelerate. Alicia lost her grip on the makeshift strap and tumbled from Fiona's back, barely avoiding crushing Mickey in the process. Faster and faster they went, as the mountain around them came to life in the form of a troll. Alicia scrambled to try and grab onto something, but as she had seen, nothing was growing here, and the only features were the giant strands of hair that looked like burned trees. It took everything in her power just to roll enough to the left or right, dodging the stiff hairs. Amazingly, she still retained her grip on the walking stick which she tried digging into the ground ahead of her. The speed of her descent was reduced slightly, but not enough to have any real effect, and she continued to plummet toward the ground below.

Fiona lunged forward, grabbing quickly for the back of Alicia's shirt. She caught it in her front teeth and dug her hooves hard into the ground. For a moment, it seemed like their slide was slowing and a quick flash of hope burned in Alicia's chest.

Suddenly, there came a loud ripping

sound and Alicia tumbled away from the deer, her shirt torn. As the hill continued to become steeper, Fiona lost her footing as well and once again began to slide downhill at a quickening pace.

It appeared there was no way to stop their descent and the bottom was quickly approaching.

"What do we do, what do we do?" Mickey, clinging as hard as he could to her flowing hair, chattered into her ear panicked like he had never been before.

"I'm sorry, I'm so, so sorry. I failed you all!" Alicia cried, doing everything in her power to avoid anything that could hurt them as her downhill momentum continued. "I dragged you along on this insane quest of mine to speak to a giant tree that is not going to listen to me anyway. And now, because of my stupid ideas, we are all going to die!"

"Be at peace, child," the voice came into her head. "Understand that sometimes you must accept fate. All the responsibility is not yours to take. Those who accompany you chose to do so willingly because you accepted them. You showed them love and what it means to care for each other. While tragic, know that you hold no fault for our deaths and no one blames you for this."

Alicia heard the deer's words even though Fiona was now well ahead of her on their frightening downhill journey. She took some comfort in the words, despite the deadly circumstance she now found herself in. Fiona was right, and in these last moments, Alicia truly understood the value of friendship. She would not have survived this long in this place without her companions. For a brief time, she had shown them that despite their differences, they could support and care for each other. She took consolation in knowing that at least Briar would escape unharmed.

As their group slid closer and closer to the base, Alicia hoped that the fall would end quickly for all of them. She did not want to survive only to have her bones ground into dust by the mountain troll's rock teeth.

From the corner of her eye, Alicia saw the earth swinging toward her. Only, looking again, she realized it wasn't the earth at all. It was a giant arm, blocking out all vision of the horizon. And attached to that arm was the most massive hand she could ever imagine. It was almost as big as her whole cabin! The hand swung toward their group and with a surprisingly delicate touch, it grabbed Alicia, Mickey, and Fiona from its massive side in one scoop. Cradled in the giant hand, they raised up through the air, higher and higher until, at last, they came to a stop far above the ground. Alicia turned and found herself looking into the most hideous face possible. She froze. While their uncontrolled fall may have stopped, and they were saved from smashing into the ground, the group of friends was a long way from being safe. And the danger staring them in the face looked much worse than the death they were anticipating only moments earlier.

"Look at all these delightfully bite-sized morsels," the mountain troll rumbled, his breath washing over the three of them like a wave of hot air. It smelled like a putrid garbage dump outside of a fishery on the most scorching of summer days. The stench was that of rotting carcasses and it choked her, causing her to cough violently. His voice sounded like stone grinding on stone, his mouth dark and huge like the largest, most frightening cavern ever seen.

"Not much of a meal exactly, but definitely worth snacking on." He smacked his huge lips for emphasis and it sounded like small explosions.

Alicia, tired from the journey, but with adrenaline coursing through her veins from the near-death experience, drew herself up to her full height and stood her ground. Her mind was full of only two thoughts: she loved her friends and would not let this monster hurt them, and she was not going to let anyone stop her from getting to Gran'tree because he was the only one left who could help her get back to her world.

"We are not afraid of you, Bristleback!" she exclaimed with power in her tired voice.

But the truth was, she was more terrified than she had ever been in her whole, entire, young life. "If you are going to eat us and grind our bones to powder, then just do it!" *Where was this coming from*, Alicia wondered, but the words just kept coming out of her mouth. "We don't want to smell your horrid breath anymore, or we may just die right here from its nastiness!" She looked closely at his stone teeth and was wracked with chills, realizing what they could do.

Bristleback's other hand came into view to her right, looking like an enormous stone hill. It was confusing to her senses to watch something so large rise into the air as if it were filled with helium and light as a feather. She could only stare, following its progress. The hand formed a fist and one huge finger extended, moving toward Alicia and her friends with speed. They tried to dodge out of the way, each moving in a different direction, but how do you avoid a wrecking ball? The finger paused in its forward progress a moment before it would have slammed into Alicia. Then it moved again, hitting her in the side with just enough force to knock her down. It was like being run over by a slow moving car, impossible to stop, and Alicia fell to her side, throwing out her hands to catch herself on the surface of the great palm she had been standing on seconds before. She looked quickly for her friends and saw that they were both okay nearby. She had no idea where Briar had flown off to, but felt a moment of happiness for him and, truth be told, a moment of envy about his wings as well. Bristleback withdrew his finger with a low chuckle. "Oh, ho, ho, so you know my name, do you, little one?" Bristleback questioned the girl. "Tell me. Do you believe that knowledge of someone's name gives you the right to insult and judge?"

Alicia lay on the stone hand where she had fallen, head bowed and her hair, dirty from endless days of travel, hung in her face. "No," she said softly, quietly. She began to tremble uncontrollably. The brief moment of fight she had drained out of her with the realization of the monster's strength, and the feeling that they would all die took hold again.

"I know many names as well, but you I have never met," the mountain troll mused. "What do they call you? It would only be polite to know who I am having for dinner."

Alicia cringed, hearing the double meaning in the troll's words. The fear settled back in stronger, but she was not ready to just give up and fought to control her shivering. If she

could talk with him, maybe she could reason with him as well. Like convincing her parents to let her watch one more show before doing her homework, or asking for thirty more minutes to play outside, even though it was starting to get dark and the streetlights had come on."My name is Alicia," she said. "And these are my friends, Mickey and Fiona." She gestured with one hand towards the two sprawled to her side, both of them staring wide-eyed and frozen. "And then there's Briar fly--" she choked on the word, a sob threatening to bubble up from her throat. "Flying somewhere close," she finished.

Bristleback's grey eyes flicked between the three of them, settling back on Alicia. "And tell me, how did such a small human-thing come to be in the Wild Side? It has been eons since your kind was last seen here. Since the barrier was formed to keep you out!"

She paused at his question, surprised he would ask and thankful for any delay of the horror to come. "I, uh, I just stepped in."

"You stepped in? Ah, then you must have some magic within you," growled Bristleback with a small note of surprise. Alicia almost felt like retching from his foul breath and focused on trying to breathe through her mouth to minimize the smell. "And if you just stepped in, why didn't you step right back out?"

"I couldn't," Alicia said, recalling the same conversation with Mickey when she first arrived. The courage Alicia showed moments before started to slip away, her confident stare turned into a familiar look of sadness. "It was gone. I turned around and it was gone." Her shoulders were no longer square and strong, they now drooped downward as if in defeat and she felt that familiar knot forming in her throat. "My dad, my mom, the cabin, the lake. Everything just gone." Tears began to form in her eyes and she angrily wiped them away. She didn't want this monster to see her cry, so she looked him directly in the eye again, trying to convince herself as much as him, that she was ready to take him on if she had to.

"I understand, little one," the troll said. "My people are gone too. I fear I am the last of my kind, alone here in this land. And now, even I am fading."

Alicia paused. Was that compassion she heard in his rocky voice? She looked closer at the giant creature and noticed patches of stone showing through his earthen skin in multiple places.

"Soon I will crumble and fall into a pile of boulders. The land is drying up, you see.

Gran'Tree is taking all the water and without it, my body is drying up too. Such is the way of things of age and magic. There is only so much water to go around and when it's gone, well..." Bristleback breathed a heavy sigh that rocked the group backward.

"But that is what I am trying to solve," Alicia said with new hope. She rose to her feet, pleading her case to the troll. "I–we–all of us are going to see the great tree. I am going to convince it that what it's doing is wrong, and that it must give back to the land instead of just taking from it."

"Silly girl, how will you convince it of such a thing? Gran'Tree has been stealing water for ages. It has grown so big, it towers over the forest and would barely even see you."

"I am tired of everyone calling me a silly girl!" Alicia said defiantly, cocking one hip in disgust. "I am no such thing! I may be young, and I may be small, but I know a great many things." She straightened her stance to face her captor and make sure Bristleback caught every word she said. "I know how it is to be a deer and run through the fields. I know how it is to be a bird and soar through the air. I know how it is to be a squirrel and hide from the great owls."

Alicia bowed her head, her voice filling with compassion. "And I know how it is to be a human and to love others, regardless of what they might look like on the outside." Her head snapped back up, staring the troll in the face. "Even if they are creatures of the forest. Even if they are giant nasty trolls with bad breath, like you!" She spoke as indignantly as she possibly could under these challenging circumstances. "I am NOT silly and I WILL speak with

Gran'Tree and he WILL hear me!"

The tears left Alicia's eyes and were replaced with a fierce strength that even surprised Bristleback. Looking deeply at her, he thought maybe, just maybe, this little human child *might* actually have a chance. He saw her determination, her strength as she fought not to cry, and her immeasurable courage as she spoke to him with such authority.

"I believe you, little one. I have lost my friends, my family. They've gone to The Drying or left for other realms. I have seen other ancient things, like the giants of old, die right in front of me. I have a sense that my own days remaining are limited."

"Then don't eat us!" Alicia begged. "Let me speak with Gran'Tree. Help me make him understand! Please, he is my only hope. The only hope for all of us!" She gestured to her friends, but included Bristleback in the swing of her arm.

A huge rumbling sound like thunder began to come from the massive troll. A strong wave of fetid air came in huffs and puffs from his cavernous mouth as the sound of thunder grew louder and more intense. She covered her ears, trying to reduce the volume that had almost become painful. Mickey and Fiona hunkered down against the onslaught of noise. Had she angered the creature?

Bristleback threw back his head and an explosion of laughter burst forth, boiling up to the skies causing sound waves that were almost visible with their intensity. His huge hand shook from the laughter and Alicia quickly sat down to avoid falling again.

After a few moments, the great laughter died down and Bristleback lowered his face to the trio. "I was never going to eat you!" he confessed, the laughter still in in voice. "Clearly you don't know anything about mountain trolls. We don't eat creatures. We eat rocks!"

"But you said..." Alicia started to argue, glancing quickly at Mickey sitting nearby. The squirrel, still quaking in fear, shrugged his little shoulders at her.

"I know what I said," the troll replied, the last of the laughter leaving his voice. "Since the rest of my kind left or died, I have preferred solitude--welcomed it even. The creatures of the forest want to believe me a monster? Let them! It allows me to be left alone, which is all I want in these final years of my life."

Alicia rose once again to her feet, rage and relief battling for dominance within her chest. "How DARE you!" she yelled, fists balled at her sides, her cheeks flaming red with heat.

"How DARE you terrify us like that! We almost DIED tumbling down your back! You held us to your face and taunted us? Said we were '*worth snacking on*'? And now you laugh at us?!" Alicia screamed her fury at the giant troll. "HOW DARE YOU!!"

Bristleback was momentarily stunned by the intense hostility coming from the young girl. He opened his mouth to speak, paused, and closed it. Looking at the girl, he again opened his mouth to speak and held his breath a moment before saying, "You are right, I am sorry. That was... unkind."

Those were not the words Alicia had expected to hear. She hesitated. The outburst had drained her, and the fury of moments before seeped away as well.

"I have let an anger build inside my chest over a great while. The Drying has taken its toll on me as much as it has the rest of the lands and the creatures within. The loss of my family has changed me. But somehow I believe you could possibly save me, too." He looked at her for a response but Alicia offered no words, mesmerized by what she was hearing, so he continued. "Maybe you could save us all. There is strength and power in you that I have never seen in one so small. Like lightning and fire behind your eyes. Perhaps it is this ability to love others not of your kind. Perhaps it is something even greater than that. I do not understand this concept 'love' you speak of, but I believe you have incredible courage in you. So, I am going to help you get to Gran'Tree. Traveling as you were would take several more days and time is short. Instead, I will carry you so we can reach the old tree by tomorrow. And then we will see what we will see." They all braced against the foul-smelling deep breath he took after that long speech.

"Oh, thank you, thank you, Bristleback!" Alicia exclaimed hopefully. She looked to her friends who stared, shocked and unbelieving, at this turn of events. They had spent a lifetime, generations in fact, in fear of this unknown monster. She knew it would take a long time for them to accept that the belief they had held so deep was nothing more than a façade, a wall Bristleback had built around himself to protect him from ever having to feel the loss of anything or anyone again.

Briar, having heard the great laughter and seeing his friends uninjured came flying cautiously up to the group. "*CAW CAW*-licia, you're still alive!"

"Yes, Briar. And it seems, with the help of Bristleback, we are very near the end of our journey."

CH. 12 CHARON BY NIGHT
(A SECRET SHARED)

Riding in the hand of the mountain troll was surprisingly comfortable. Alicia found the stone-like skin to have a slight give to it, like the firmest of mattresses. Standing and looking out across the lands from this height, her hand gripping one of the stony fingers as best she could for balance, Alicia was amazed at how vast the forest truly was. This must be what it is like for the hawks and vultures that soar high above the treetops in their hunt for food. The wind was stronger up here and blew her hair out behind her. Mickey rode on her shoulder, taking comfort from the girl, still trembling a bit from fright of both the troll carrying them and from being so high in the air. He had climbed trees before, but never very high. He was mostly a ground-dwelling squirrel. Fiona had tried to stand as well, but the constant movement of Bristleback's hand made the deer unsteady, so she chose to re-main lying down, legs curled underneath her, peering through the gaps between his massive fingers to watch their progress.

From this vantage, Alicia could also see

how far and wide The Drying had spread. She saw large, dark brown trails, like tendrils reaching out from some unseen place far ahead. The Drying radiated outward from each of these tendrils, sucking the life-giving water from the soil and plants in the vicinity. It was terrifying to see and served to reinforce the urgency of what they hoped to accomplish.

She lowered herself back down to a sitting position. The way Bristleback's fingers curled up to cradle them, which sent chills up her spine the first time he did, was just right so that she could lie against any one of them as a backrest to relieve the ache of many days traveling on Fiona. Admittedly, deer-back riding was not the most comfortable way to go, especially for one with no riding experience.

"How are you feeling, Mickey?" she asked the small squirrel, sensing that he couldn't quite shake his caution and apprehension. Alicia felt bad for him and wanted to lead by example and show that they could trust the mountain troll, even though she herself still felt some of the lingering fear. After all, even if a mountain lion told you she wouldn't eat you, would you ever really feel comfortable? "This is kind of amazing, right?" she said to break the silence.

"Amazing. Yeah. Sure." Mickey, climbing down from her shoulder to sit on her lap, did not sound convinced. "I do appreciate the quick travel, especially for you, but do you really think he *only* eats rocks? That doesn't sound right to me. Rocks?!?"

"I trust him, Mickey," Alicia said with more confidence than she felt. "It sounds like he has lost a lot and has been suffering for a long time." She looked up at the troll's face, craggy and ancient, his eyes remaining focused toward a destination they could not yet see. "I understand him. I have only been separated from my family for a short time now and it has been difficult. I don't know what I would have done if I had been alone, without Fiona to help with travel and Briar to help with finding food, but especially you, Mickey." She looked back at the little squirrel. "You were my first connection to any living thing here in this world. You accepted me and helped me from the beginning, no questions asked. I love you for that."

She reached down to stroke the top of his head. "Stop that now," he said gruffly, brushing her fingers away with one hand while trying to brush away a tear with the other without being noticed. Alicia saw, but didn't say anything.

"Speaking of food, I'm hungry." Mickey

said with a quick sniffle. "Can you get this ugly, lumbering beast to set us down for a bit so we can find something to eat?"

"Now, now, Mickey, there's no need for name calling," she scolded lightly. Turning her face back toward the troll she called to him. "Bristleback? Could you please put us down for a moment near that stream over there?" she asked, pointing. "We are getting quite hungry and I imagine that Fiona would love the chance to stand for a bit." She sent an image of standing on the ground near the water to Fiona and saw the deer's eyes light up with anticipation.

"Certainly, little one," Bristleback rumbled back. A few long strides carried them to the stream, still out of range of the dark tendrils. The troll gently lowered the group and they clambered out of his hand to the ground.

Fiona stretched her legs, sending a grateful image of comfort and relief to Alicia.

"Look, huckleberries!" Mickey exclaimed, scampering for the small bush close at hand and, eagerly picking berries, stuffing them into his mouth with glee. Alicia laughed at his antics, moving toward the bush herself. This one was loaded with ripe, purple berries and she dug in. Briar came flying down through the branches as well, joining them for the small feast.

"We are traveling so *CAW* fast now it is a challenge for me to *CAW* keep up!" Briar announced as Alicia tossed a few berries to him. "We will get to Gran'Tree in *CAW* no time at all!"

"Yes we will, Briar, and I want to thank you for staying with us and keeping us company," Alicia responded, gratitude in her voice, her teeth and tongue stained purple from the berry juice. "I know you don't have to, but your presence here is welcomed and wanted."

"It has been an interesting *CAW* journey, for sure, scary even, but fun!" Briar shrieked in his raucous voice. Alicia looked at the bird and even though he may not have been able to smile, his beak being solid and all, she could see the pleasure shining in his dark eyes. "I told you before that my *CAW*-ind are used to traveling alone, unlike my cousins, so this has *CAW* been unique and surprisingly enjoyable. Even in the *CAW*-ompany of that ratty old squirrel!"

"Hey now," Mickey retorted, "who are you calling ratty? You come over here! I'll pull out a few of those feathers and then we'll see who's ratty!" Alicia chuckled at the exchange, watching the smile never leave Mickey's face and knowing the words were in jest.

Fiona chewed on some leaves from a nearby bush and then walked off toward the stream to get a drink of fresh water. Alicia moved to join her.

"And you too," she thought to the deer. "You offered to carry me, yet with the help of the troll, you still remain. I appreciate your company as well."

"As I said when we met, your story moved me. Bristleback was right when he said there is a strength in you. I don't know if this is common in all humans, but I am thrilled to know you," she sent Alicia an image of the flying machine they discussed before, "and learn of your world. I believe you have done something incredible here, bringing together this unlikely band of creatures." Alicia saw in her mind an image of all of them riding in Bristleback's hand with Briar flying close. "I am unaccus-tomed to spending time with any creatures outside of my own family and herd. This has been a challenge I never would have imagined before. You were an unknown, young one, but I saw in you a kindness." Fiona projected an image of the two of them lying in a meadow, the warm sun shining down on their bodies. "I took a chance with you and it has been an extraordinary honor to be a part of this grand journey. If anyone can talk to Gran'Tree and be heard, it is you. I will be with you until the end."

Alicia leaned forward and wrapped her arms around the deer's neck, feeling the rough hair against her cheek. "I hope you're right, Fiona. I really do."

The sun sank behind what was left of the tree line as the night sky set in and, even with the moon creeping slowly over the horizon, Alicia found that she could not sleep. Anxiety about the upcoming meeting with an unknown giant tree with a reputation for being unsympathetic swept through her mind. She thought of all the ways it could go wrong. What if the tree didn't see her? What if it didn't listen? Surely with the help of her new friends--Fiona, Mickey, Briar, and now especially Bristleback--the tree *must* take notice of her. But would he hear her words? And even if he did, would he be bothered enough care? After all, Mickey had told her that many of the forest creatures had tried to plead their cases and failed. If Gran'Tree didn't listen, well then maybe they could force him to comply. *I mean, we have a mountain troll on our side!!* Alicia thought. *He could just rip that big old tree right out of the ground, couldn't he?* Her worried mind could not stop thinking, but her tired body needed rest. Alicia knew she had to be her best self tomorrow and that a good night's sleep would help, but she felt like she was crossing the river Styx and that Bristleback was her ferryman.

The others were asleep, Fiona's legs curled tightly underneath her with her nose tucked into the bend, and Mickey resting close by, his nose twitching from whatever squirrel dreams were spinning through his head. Briar, who had saved Mickey's life and possibly even Alicia's, was barely visible draped in his black and blue feathers. He was resting on the tip of one of the giant fingers on Bristleback's dark hand, his head tucked under one wing. The forest creatures had taken a bit longer to trust the mountain troll than the human child, having lived their entire lives fearing him. But as sky blue transitioned into sky black, and the moon rose over the nearby hills, their stress diminished as friendly conversation led them to acceptance. Now, watching them sleep, Alicia felt closer to them than ever. They had been good traveling companions these past several days. Better than good, they had been wonderful and kind. But she knew their time together may be coming to an end. If everything turned out the way they hoped, tomorrow she would be back home with her human family. She would miss all of these new friends of hers, terribly.

"Bristleback," she whispered into the night. The wind had died down and in the quiet of the dark her words carried more clearly.

"Yes, little one, should you not be sleeping like the others?" Bristleback kept his head turned away so as not to bother her with the smell of his breath. Alicia was surprised by his consideration, given that he was a troll. She was appreciative as well.

"I have a secret. I haven't told the others because I was worried if I did, it might not come true. You know, like a birthday wish or something."

"I have carried many secrets over my long lifetime. Soon, I will be gone. Like all the ancient ruins of the lands that hold their own mysteries, your secret will be safe with me."

Alicia looked at him and could see it was true. The light in Bristleback's eyes was dimmer than before; she had gotten a good look at them when she faced him in fear earlier in the day. More stone was visible under his blue-grey skin, too. Alicia knew she must convince Gran'Tree to release the water, if only to save this once frightening monster. She must help him and the others! Bristleback had seemed to act so cruelly all the time and made everyone fear him, but he wasn't bad at all, really. He was just alone. And like her and the rest of her traveling companions, he simply needed a family to support and care about him.

"I am going to ask Gran'Tree to help me return to my world. To be so powerful, he must have very old magic, right? If anyone could do that for me, I'll bet he could."

"You may be right, little one. His magic is immeasurably strong. I could not defeat him, even if I still had the strength of youth to call on."

"Do you really think he will listen to me?" she asked, gazing hopefully at her giant friend.

"I think if anyone has a chance to be heard, it is you. You fought the predators who wanted to eat the squirrel, even tamed a bird and rode the four-legged beast. And somehow, you got this old troll with bad breath to listen to you. You have given me hope, child, something that has been rare in my life. Tomorrow, we will do whatever it takes to make him listen. What he chooses to do after that will be up to him. Just know that regardless of what happens, you have done the best you could."

"Thank you, Bristleback." Alicia felt a calmness take over her worried mind. "Thank you for everything."

"You are welcome, little one. Now go to sleep. I will get us there safely tonight, you have no need to fear. Tomorrow is a big day."

"And Bristleback?"

"Yes, little one?"

"Thank you for not eating us."

"You are welcome, little one. You would not have made much of a meal anyway. And you're too squishy."

Alicia smiled at that. She lay her head down and closed her eyes. The mountain troll was right. Tomorrow would be the biggest day of her life.

CH. 13 JOURNEY'S END

"Alicia, look! Alicia!"

Alicia opened her eyes because Mickey would not stop jabbering. She reluctantly lifted her head from the great hand of Bristleback, ready to yell at the squirrel to be quiet, only to see him hopping up and down while pointing off to the distance. Fiona and Briar were already awake and looking in the same direction.

"It's *CAW* massive! I could fly up and up and up and get *CAW* tired before I ever reached the top!"

Alicia looked to where they were pointing and saw it. An immense tree on the horizon, reaching all the way up to the heavens. The top of the tree was lost among the low-hanging clouds. It was almost impossible to comprehend how anything could be so huge.

As they came over the top of a small mountain and looked down into the valley below, they could see the vast dead clearing where shade from the massive tree killed anything that attempted to grow. Beyond that, the dry land extended even further, and small dust devils could be seen whirling their brief dances across the ground, disappearing back into the dirt, only to be born again like phoenixes somewhere else on the landscape.

"It is as I feared, young one," Fiona spoke her silent language to Alicia. "It is why I left this place. The Drying is spreading more rapidly than expected. It won't be long before there is no more water left in the entire Wild Side. There can be no grazing because grasslands cannot exist without water."

Mickey ran up to Alicia's shoulder to get a better view. "We need to put a stop to this now," he said pointing a tiny finger determinedly at the giant tree.

"Let's get down there, Bristleback," Alicia said. "Let's end this."

As they moved down into the valley, the great tree loomed larger and larger above them. It was truly was a sight to behold. Its

trunk was so wide, even Bristleback would not have been able to wrap his arms around it.

Alicia saw now that any thoughts of forcing Gran'Tree to do what they wanted were simply foolish ideas. She remembered seeing pictures of skyscrapers in books about New York City. Gran'Tree was just as big, maybe even bigger than the tallest building.

They stepped into the clearing and Bristleback came to a stop. "I must rest, little one. The night's journey has taken its toll on me and I can feel a change in my bones."

He gently lowered the group to the ground, and then sat next to them, shaking the ground with a thump as he did. Alicia could see the weariness in his craggy features, the glow in his eyes was even more distant than the night before.

"That's okay, Bristleback. We are almost

at an end to our journey. It is probably good to have a moment to prepare our thoughts."

"I fear my own journey truly *is* at an end," Bristleback grumbled softly. He could no longer sit upright and collapsed to his side, catching himself with one arm. "I think I might just lie down here for a while and watch the sky." Bristleback laid his head against the ground.

"What are you saying, Bristleback?" asked Alicia, fearful of his answer.

Bristleback turned his head towards the girl. "All things come to an end, little one. Even ancient things like me. I am the last of my kind in this land. It was only a matter of time before The Drying claimed me as well."

Tears welled up in Alicia's eyes. "But we are so close! Just stay with us a few hours more. I know I can save you. I can save everyone!"

"I believe you can, little one, I believe you can. But my time here is done. Even now, I can feel my bones changing." Bristleback's eyes squinted against the pain before his features relaxed once more. "Don't be sad, I've lived a long life. Now GOOO!" he mustered all of the strength he could find to growl one more strong command. Its power caused a familiar rumble of the earth below. "Make the tree answer for what he has done to this land." Alicia stumbled and fell to her knees with the shaking of the ground.

"But I don't know what to do," she sobbed, pain in her knees, afraid for her friend, and suddenly confronted with the weight of all she had to do. "Gran'Tree is so big, bigger than I ever imagined. How can I possibly get his attention? How can I make him listen to me? I need you, Bristleback!" She reached out and placed a hand against the stone cheek of the troll, feeling the cold, rough skin of his face. "I need your size and strength. We all do."

Without opening his eyes, exhausted from the effort to send them on their way, he whispered, "you have more size and strength in you than you know, little one. You have a great power. You conquered even me. You helped me let go of my anger and find friendship again, even if for a short time."

The mountain troll paused, his breathing deep and slow. One huge hand raised to rub at the newly formed rock appearing from under the skin of his head, then dropped back to the ground with an earth-shaking tremor, causing Fiona and Mickey to take a few steps backwards. "You are so willing to accept others without judgment," he spoke again. "Your compassion for all things softened even my hard skin. I think … maybe … I even understand this love you talked about."

Bristleback found the strength to open his eyes and looked intently at her. She could see his skin changing rapidly now, drying out, turning from the blue-grey of their first meeting to the dusty grey color of stone. "Little one," he spoke, his voice pitched so low now that only she could hear. "As I promised, your secret is safe with me. But I believe you should tell the others. They are your friends. They care for you and they need to know. You should not have to struggle with this alone. They can help you."

"You're right," Alicia cried softly, watching this mountain of strength become weaker and weaker, his body at last succumbing to the awfulness of The Drying. "I will. I promise."

"You gave me a greater purpose at the end

of my life. For that I am grateful. I will carry your memory to the next land." Bristleback paused, looking at the human child beside him. "I was wrong," he whispered. "Ending this life alone would have been a terrible thing. I was blind for many years, but I see now. Even with our short acquaintance, I am thankful to have known you. Where I am going I will tell all of the human child who called me 'friend.' Now leave me and go do what you came here to do. I have faith in you. Believe in yourself, Alicia. You will find a way."

"I will remember you, always," Alicia cried softly, looking into the large grey eyes of the troll. "Thank you, Bristleback. Thank you."

With a final sigh, Bristleback closed his eyes. His face hardened in the dry air, freezing his craggy features in place. As she watched, the mountain troll slowly crumbled into pieces, leaving behind nothing but a huge pile of stone. A memorial to forever mark the passing of this last ancient creature. Her friend.

CH. 14 A CHOICE IS MADE

Alicia stared at the pile of boulders where once her friend sat, and felt anger building inside of her. It was completely unfair, to get so close, only to lose Bristleback now. How dare Gran'Tree be so selfish!

Alicia wiped her tears away and looked

to her friends, who came closer now to provide comfort in her moment of sorrow. Even though they had been terrified at the thought of meeting Bristleback, their fear was replaced with compassion and understanding for the massive being that had carried them to the end of their journey. He had a gentle way which they had never anticipated. They, too, felt the pain of his loss. Each of their lives would be forever changed from the short time spent with the troll.

Fiona knelt gently once again so that Alicia could climb on her back. She grabbed the strap and balanced herself astride the deer just as she had done before. Alicia could not resist one last look back at what remained of her friend, and a determination grew within her. With Mickey on her shoulder and Briar flying above, they moved forward to meet the great tree and demand that he answer for what he had done to their home.

Entering into the shade of the large branches, Alicia felt the air temperature drop. Whereas the surrounding climate felt like a warm day in summer, underneath the giant branches it was more like a cool spring morning. Alicia pulled the towel, dirty from travel, from Fiona's back and wrapped it tightly around her shoulders. Mickey pressed up against her neck and her first companion in this land was now a small spot of warmth against the cold.

As they approached the great tree, more details began to take shape. She could see that it was a giant yellow pine. Its bark was covered in what looked like enormous puzzle pieces, all stuck randomly together. The floor of the clearing was littered with large, heavy looking pine cones and she could see the ground bulging, where the tree's massive roots extended outwards, pushing up the earth. These must be the source of the great tendrils of darkness she had seen earlier, increasing their reach out into the lands to absorb every last bit of water.

Stopping several yards from the trunk of the enormous tree, Alicia climbed down from the back of the deer and looked at her companions. Bristleback's final words came back to her.

"I need to tell you something," Alicia said. These friends, her family in this realm, looked at her–waiting. "I am going to ask Gran'Tree to open the barrier and send me home. I don't know if he will, or even if he can, but I need to try and return to my own life. I will miss you all dearly. You mean more to me than you will ever know. But I miss my parents. I miss my friends. I miss my school. I miss the cabin and the lake. If this works, this may be my last chance to say goodbye." She paused to give Mickey the opportunity to climb onto her hand so that she could look at him, Fiona, and Briar. "Please take care of each other."

She turned to Fiona, patting the deer's soft neck while she listened. "Good luck to you, young one," Fiona spoke in her usual silent way. "I am happy that I could help bring you here. You taught me many things I will never forget, like hearing of the mechanical birds and seeing the images you shared with me of your other home." Fiona sent one final image to Alicia. It was of a large buck, with many pronged antlers, standing high on a snow-covered hill overlooking a valley.

"Your father?" Alicia asked.

"I too know what it is to miss our parents,"

Fiona acknowledged. "Now go back to yours, but never forget that you have friends here."

Alicia was filled with a feeling of love and grace. She turned away from Fiona to find Briar looking at her.

"*CAW*! Thank you for sharing your songs with me. I will never *CAW* sing them as well as you, but I will *CAW*-arry them with me, always!"

"You have a wonderful singing voice, Briar," Alicia said. "Don't let anyone tell you different. And don't let that furball of a squirrel boss you around. You are handsome, proud, and brave. You saved my life and I will always be thankful for that. I promise that if I make it home, I will always leave out extra peanuts for your brothers and sisters in my world."

"I will *CAW* miss you, Alicia. You have helped me understand that *CAW* there are more important things than just me in this *CAW* world. Though my *CAW*-ind are used to fending for ourselves, I promise never to be selfish again!"

Alicia turned back to Mickey, who was now on Fiona's back where he climbed when Alicia petted the doe's warm neck. He was her first companion in this land and her dearest friend in this place.

"It was my great honor to meet a human," Mickey said. "I hope that all humans are as kind as you. It has been a real pleasure." He quickly turned away, but not before she saw a small tear slide down his fuzzy cheek.

She leaned over to pick him up. "Stop that now, or you are going to make me cry again, too," she sniffled. "I will never forget you, Mickey. I have learned so much from you. You've been one of my best friends in the whole world. Watch over these two when I'm gone." She stroked Fiona and looked up at the jay, who had perched on a low branch. "Don't let Briar steal all the food. And Fiona may be quiet, but she has a wonderful soul. Keep them close and be kind to each other, that's what we call 'love' back home. It's the best thing you can do."

"I'm not a furball, by the way."

"No, Mickey, no you're not. You are bigger than you know. Stay strong, my furry friend."

She took her friend, and squatting, lowered Mickey back to the ground, gave him a final scratch on his head, and then she stood. One by one she hugged the others as gently as she could, one final time. The lost traveler never would have made it this far without them, and she loved each one for the support they had given her.

"Now, let's get this done."

Alicia approached Gran'Tree on foot, stepping over and around the roots exploding out of the ground like giant sewer pipes, massive and swollen with the water they channeled to the tree. In truth, it was a grand tree, towering over the clearing. This close, she could see ants and centipedes carving their separate paths through the large crevices in the bark. Looking up, her eyes searched as high as possible, and still she could barely make out his face. From this distance, the eyes appeared to be giant cracks in the great puzzle bark, looking out and surveying all that he ruled. She yelled up to him.

"Hey! Hey, you! Gran'Tree! HEEEYYYYY!!"

Her voice carried, it was soft yet forceful, but the great tree simply ignored her.

"HEEYYYY!! HELLO!!! I'M DOWN HERE!!"

She put more energy into her call, but again, there was no response. It was as Mickey had told her, so long ago. The tree either could not hear, or was simply choosing to ignore. Maybe to it, she sounded like an annoying yappy dog.

"Let me *CAW* try!" Briar screeched. He launched himself skyward, dodging branches and flying up as hard as he could, while the rest of the group waited down below.

Higher and higher he flew, his wings tired, but Briar was determined to get the old tree's attention.

"*CAW CAW CAW*!" Briar continued to screech, until finally coming level with the tremendous face of the yellow pine. "*CAW CAW CAW CAW*!!"

"Gooo awaayyyy, youuu annoooyyinggg liittlllee gnaaat." Gran'Tree spoke in a voice that was deep and slow, carrying across this clearing and the valley beyond. His face crackled and crunched with the movement of his speech. His mouth was a huge gash across the trunk, as if some giant lumberjack long ago had swung his axe a few times and removed a chunk of the old tree. In some years past, sap had dripped from the corners of the mouth and dried into two long yellow and amber streaks, like frozen streams. His huge eyes were two knots uneven in size and above the gash. They looked older than anything Briar could imagine. They were rimmed with greenish moss. "Youuu arrreee distuurbiiinggg meee."

"*CAW CAW CAW*!!" Briar responded. He looked into the eyes of Gran'Tree and Briar could see himself reflected in something shiny right in the middle of those big knots. He remembered Alicia's words. *He was proud. He was brave.* "I will NOT *CAW* LEAVE!!"

"Whyyy dooo youuu insiiist oonnninnter-ruuuptiiingg myyyy reessst?"

"There is someone *CAW* below that needs to speak with you!" Briar shrieked.

"Aaannd whyyy shouuuld Iiii speeeak wiiith aaanyyyooonnne?"

"It's a human CAW child!"

"Aaa huuummaaan chiiillld?" Gran'Tree turned his immense eyes downward and saw the small being, waving frantically from below. "Innnterrressstiiinnng. Veeerrryyy weeelllll. Iiii wiiillll liiisteeennn."

Alicia stood in awe of the giant tree, feeling the vibrations from the tremendous voice course through her very bones. With its attention focused on her, she found herself completely tongue-tied, her former confidence draining away. What could she possibly say to this *thing* that would make it listen? She was small, insignificant, and nothing compared to the grandeur of this being. She glanced back at her friends, both trembling in fear at being this close to the massive yellow pine but wanting to stay near to their human friend and provide support.

"Hello, uh, Mr. Gran'Tree. My name is Alicia," she spoke timidly.

"Speeeaaak loouuudeeerrr. Iii caannn baaarelyyy heeeaaarrr youuu," the tree spoke, undisguised boredom in his voice

Turning her head upward and cupping her small hands around the sides of her mouth like a megaphone, she used her voice as loud as she ever had in her life. Even louder than when she'd call her dad to dinner standing on the dock while he was in the middle of the lake, fishing in the rowboat. "Believe in yourself, Alicia," Bristleback had said. "You will find a way." She repeated the words, "My name is Alicia. And I have traveled a long, long way to talk to you. Why are you taking all the water?"

"Whyyy shouuuldnnn't Iii taaake aaallll theee waaateerrr? Waaateeerrr iiisss poooweeerrr. Aaannnd Iii ammm theee mooosst poooweeerrfuulll ooofff aaallll."

Alicia felt her blood getting hot as the anger grew inside of her. "Can't you see what you are doing to the land? You are literally killing all the plants and creatures who live there! You killed my friend! Bristleback was the very last of the mountain trolls. You drove away or killed the rest of his family with your water stealing, and now you have killed him as well!" She shouted at the tree even louder, with fury in her voice.

"Waaasss thaaaat theee giiiaaant whooo enteeerreed myyy valllleeeyyy? Iii saaawww hiiimm faaalllll." The lack of concern was apparent in the tree's voice, as if he was speaking of watching a flower wilt.

"Yes," she screamed, her face as red as her aching throat felt. "And it's all your fault! His name was Bristleback and YOU killed him! You killed him and you are killing the land, and soon, all of us. We will all be dead and gone and you'll be alone. Who will you rule over then, huh? WHO??"

"Iiit maaatteeerrss nooot. Iii waaas heeer-rre aaat theee beegiiinnninnngg. Iii wiiillll beee heeerrre aaat theee eeennnd."

"What gives you the right to decide that?" the young girl asked incredulously, anger burning through her.

"Theee treeesss aarrree theee mooost anciiieeennt oooff beeeiiinggss, aaannd Iii aaammm theee graaandeeesst oooff theeemm alllll," Gran'Tree proclaimed, his huge branches creaked as they stretched outward, raining down loose pine needles on Alicia and her friends. "Thaaat giiivvvesss mmmeee aaalllll theee rrriiight Iii neeeed toooo doooo whaaat Iii waaannnt!"

Alicia was reminded of the bully in her school at home. He was the biggest kid in her grade, and because of this, he felt everyone should bow before him, like he was a king or something. It was terrible, and it made her furious to see. Well this tree was majestic all right, but he was no king. A good king would rule with a kind hand.

"You're nothing but a bully," she screamed at him, "and you have no respect for anybody but yourself! You feel you can just take because you deserve it? You deserve nothing!"

Suddenly, one of the great roots thrashed up underneath the feet of Alicia and flung her several feet into the air. She landed with little grace on her rear end, setting off a fresh round of tears at the sudden pain and humiliation.

"Hooowww DAAARRRE youuu speeeaak tooo mmmeee aaabooouuut taaakiiinng aaan-nyyythiiinnng!" Gran'Tree said menacingly. "Fooorrr yeeeaarrrsss yooouuurrr kiiinnnd tooook whaaat waaasss nnnooot theeeirrrsss." Gran'Tree's voice grew louder with fury, sending her friends scurrying back several feet. "Wwweee baaannniiisheeed youuu. Nooowww theee aaanciieeennnt ooonnneeesss aaarrre weeeaak aaannnd Iii haaavvve theee streeen-nngth. Buuut youuu dooo nooot beeelooonggg iiinnn thiiis wooorrld aaanyyymooorrre,

huuummaaan chiiillld!" The massive roots continued to quiver around the girl as if daring her to rise.

"I know that!" Alicia moaned, voice weak and rough from screaming.

"Whyyy dooonnn't youuu gooo hooommmmeee? Yooouuurrr kiiinnnd iiisss nooot weeelllcooommmed heeerrre."

"I can't!" she cried. "There's no way back. I looked and my world disappeared as soon as I stepped through into this Wild Side. My parents are gone. My life is gone. And I am alone."

His fury now spent, the great tree's roots stopped their undulating movements. "Theeerreee iisss nooo sooorrrooowww iinnn beeeiinggg alooonnneee. Iii haaaveee beeennnn alooonnneee foorrr sooo looonggg." The slightest note of compassion entered his voice. "Buuut iiff youuu waaannt, Iii caaannn seeennnd youuu baaack."

Alicia froze at those words. *Did she hear correctly?* Did Gran'Tree just say he could send her back? She hadn't dared to ask yet, fearing the answer. But now, a flame she was cautious to give life to began to bloom inside of her.

"How can you do such a thing?" she asked, hoping against hope that it was true.

"Aaasss Iii tooollld youuu, waaateerrr iiisss poooweeerrr. Aaannnd Iii aaammm fiiillled wiiith waaateerr. Iiit wiiilll nnnooot taaakee tooo muuuch, buuut Iii caaann oop- eeenn aaa paaath baaack. Youuu annnoooyyy mmeee, hhhuuummmaaannn chiiillld, aaannnd youuurrr kiiinnnd doooeesss nooot deeessseerrve tooo beee heeerrree. Iii ww- wiiilll gggllllaaadlllyy ssseeennnd youuu hooommmeee. Iii caaannn aaallwaaayyyss reeepllaaaccce theee waaateeerrr Iii uuussse."

Alicia thought about this, the flame in her chest growing brighter. She could go home, back to her family. She could see her mom and dad again! She could have her whole life back. But what would she be leaving behind? Would she be abandoning her friends in a time of need? Would she be dooming this world to death? After all, if Gran'Tree used his water to create a path to send her home, he would just draw more water from the land. Would that accelerate The Drying?

Alicia looked back at her friends, Mickey, Briar, and Fiona. They trusted her and got her here, even fighting off predators with no sign of selfishness. She looked past them to the clearing beyond to the huge pile of stones that was once the great mountain troll Bristleback, the last of his kind. What was his sacrifice for, if not to help save this world? She looked beyond even that and saw the dying lands as far as she could see. She thought of her own forest back home, so vibrant, green, and filled with life. She couldn't let The Drying continue here. She couldn't abandon this world. Not after everything she and her friends had gone through.

She knew what she had to do.

CH. 15 RAINSONG

A hush fell over the clearing and surrounding woods, as if every living thing, plant and animal alike, held its breath waiting to hear Alicia's response. She rose to her feet, brushing off the dirt from her bottom, and stepped once again toward the great trunk of the tree.

But instead of speaking, Alicia began to sing. Her voice tentative and small, she sang the melody sweet and true. *"Caring for the ones we love both family and friends. Will never be a wasted cause, and never needs to end."* The words from the song she used to sing with her father came back to her. *"The beauty of the world we see, can only grow so bright".* The tree watched her carefully, curiously listening to the music that floated up from this small human child far below it on the forest floor. *"Without the love we get and give to hold us through the night."*

As she reached the second verse, the words began flowing with more confidence, and Alicia's voice grew stronger, finding the rhythm of the verse and gaining a deeper understanding of the meaning. It was a song of love, but more than that, it was a song of compassion and of care. In the words was a truth she had always known, but only really understood here, during her time in this realm, with this strange bunch of friends she called family. The untapped magic within her gave the words power. She sang of promises and faith. Of kindness, and support. It was a song she'd heard since infancy; she knew it so well. Her voice carried up through the branches of the tall, tall tree.

A crack of lightning flashed across the sky, followed closely by a great boom of thunder rolling through the valley. In that moment, she felt the smallest drop land in her hair. Her trio of friends startled and looked quickly around for shelter. Finding none, Mickey and Briar crouched beneath Fiona's legs. The deer lowered her body a bit, protective of the smaller creatures.

Alicia showed no concern for the flash, lost in the power of the music. She lifted her face skyward and sang with all her might. *"Take a moment look around and see who needs a hand. On this shore where we exist, we're all just grains of sand."*

The giant yellow pine, so majestic and so big compared to all the other puny trees in the forest, could not hold back. The sheer beauty of this young child's voice was beyond anything he had ever heard. The birdsong in the trees could not compete. The rush of the wind through its branches could not compete. How could one so young have words to describe such wonder? Understanding slowly dawned on Gran'Tree, and with it came tears. The one thing he had all around him but didn't see.

Family.

His family was the lodge pines and the

grand fir trees. The Steller's jays and the hummingbirds. The squirrels in the trees and the chipmunks on the ground; the deer, the bears, and the owls. He had always felt alone, and so chose to *rule* instead of *love*. But the old tree was surrounded by family this entire time and all he needed was this sweet, sweet child to show him.

How selfish he had been. How blind. He cried for the sorrow he felt about what he had done, for the sadness of friends lost, and for the beauty and promise of hope that Alicia sang of. He looked out upon the boulders that used to be Bristleback, the final resting spot of the last remaining mountain troll that would forever be a reminder of what he had done. The giant pine wailed harder, knowing his actions had caused such grief. The tears flew wildly now, his massive branches shaking and stirring up the wind, his tremendous sobs booming out like thunder.

Gran'Tree's tears came down in a great storm over the forest, soaking the land as far as the eye could see, his great power was draining away and back into the world around him. The small bushes and plants bent under the torrent of rain and wind, eagerly soaking up the life-giving water. Lakes and ponds began to fill, and the frogs and salamanders which had burrowed underneath the earth so long ago started to emerge. With eyes turned to the sky, their hardened skin softened once again in the rain. Birds rubbed against the wet leaves, gathering water against their feathers and fluffing them out like they had not done in years, flinging away years of heavy dust that had begun to take a toll on their ability to fly.

In the middle of it all stood Alicia, at

the base of the giant tree, she herself lost in tears thinking about her own sacrifice and the family she would never see again. Her dad, who would play guitar and tell stupid jokes thinking he was the most hilarious person in the world. The person who would chop wood to build grand fires in the cabin fireplace and roast marshmallows perfectly, just the way she liked them. And her mom, who would always be there when she wasn't feeling well, always making her chicken noodle soup when Alicia needed it. The person who read to her at night and always had a mug of hot chocolate waiting when she came in from the cold.

And she cried for Bristleback, who gave the last of his life to get her to this spot, here and now, just moments too late to save himself.

Her upturned face and hair were soaked,

days of dirt and grime sluiced away under the torrent of rain but still, she continued with the song. Despite the storm raging around her, her voice was strong and true, reaching the final crescendo and holding the last note like she and her father always did.

As the final words left her mouth and the tones faded, Alicia felt drained. Standing there, with rain pouring down on her, she knew that she had succeeded in her quest to save the land. Gran'Tree was actually shrinking in size as great stores of water left him and flooded the landscape. She was happy for Mickey, Fiona, Briar, and all the life that would continue to thrive here on the Wild Side. But her happiness was dimmed with the understanding that by saving this land, she would never return to the life she knew.

Alicia thought of her friends, her school, and how about much she missed her mom and dad. She longed to be with them even if just to relieve their suffering at not knowing what had happened to their little girl. Now they would grow old, never learning of the adventures she had here. Never knowing all that she learned about this forest and the creatures that inhabited it. They would never get to hold their daughter again, comfortable and warm on their lap in front of the fire with the scent of wood smoke filling the air. They would never see her grow up, graduate from college, and become the young woman they knew she would become.

Alicia turned from the great tree, her eyes still filled with tears, and saw her father, kneeling in the distant bushes. His head hung low as if all the weight of the world lay on his shoulders.

"Dad? Dad?? DAD!!"

CH. 16 A BEAUTIFUL REUNION

Kneeling in the storm, Richard heard a faint voice and looked up to see movement beyond the bushes. *Was that? It couldn't be.* He had looked and looked to no avail. "Alicia!" He jumped to his feet.

Alicia ran to him through the bushes, ignoring the small scratches they made on her legs, throwing herself into his arms. Sobbing, they held each other fiercely. Alicia could barely breathe. Richard pulled away and looked at her questioningly. "Where were you? I looked and called, over and over. I was terrified I'd lost you!"

"Dad, how?" she cried, holding his hand tight with both of hers. "I was on the Wild Side," she dropped his hand and gestured toward the magnitude of the massive pine, "and Gran'Tree had sucked up all the water! He forced me to make a choice. So, I chose to save the land instead of coming home. I'm sorry, I knew it would be hard on you and Mom, but it was the right thing to do." She turned to show him where she had left the giant tree and the mysterious land behind. She froze. It was gone! The clearing, the boulders of Bristleback, a final reminder of his existence, the massive yellow pine that dominated the landscape, her friends—all gone.

"Alicia, what are you talking about? The Wild Side? Gran'Tree?"

"But Dad, it was all right there! I've been on the craziest adventure, with Mickey guiding me. I spent the night in an underground burrow and I battled foxes and one time I even slept in the hand of a mountain troll. I walked forever, and everything was dying. I had to sing, and I thought I'd never see you or Mom again!"

"Adventure? Mickey?" he took his daughter's shoulders gently, turning her to face him. "What is this nonsense? You've only been gone a few minutes," her father said incredulously as he let her go.

"What? NO, I haven't!"

"Fine, fine, let's talk about it later. I'm just glad you are safe, honey. Please don't ever go wandering off without saying anything again. Now let's find someplace dry to wait out the rest of this storm."

The storm passed quickly, as many summer storms do. Their clothes and towels were soaking wet, so there was nothing to do but dry out under the sun which had broken through the remnants of clouds left behind by the departing storm. The wind had died down as well, making the row back home easier than anticipated.

During the return trip across the lake, Alicia told her father everything: about stepping into the other world, meeting Mickey, and learning about Gran'Tree. She told of the lake disappearing, of not being able to find him, and of being cold and scared. Stories of fighting foxes, Briar, and poor old Bristleback flowed from her. Through it all, Richard listened, seeing his daughter's bright, sparkling eyes, unable to avoid her enthusiasm, and doing his best to steady the boat as she gestured wildly during the recounting of the story, especially in her recounting of the battle against the foxes. She looked like an amateur fencer, lunging forward as if her walking stick, discarded now, had been a sword.

The stories reminded her father of his own adventures as a child. He told her he would imagine that a giant log was really a crocodile, or that the moss in the trees was a sign of witches that flew through the forest at night, getting their hair caught in the branches.

"I will allow you this adventure, Alicia," he said, gesturing with the handle of the oar in her direction. "Your stories make me long for the imagination I had back when I was a child, but next time don't lose track of time so easily!"

"I bet mom is going to be really worried about us, dad!" Alicia suddenly remembered how concerned her mother had been about them rowing across the lake in the first place. She would be able to see them coming back across the lake. Alicia and Richard looked forward to the warm mugs of hot chocolate they knew would be waiting for them when they arrived. "I can't wait to get home and tell her all about Mickey, Fiona, Briar, and Bristleback. I may not tell her about Gran'Tree; he might be way too scary for her. Do you think she'll have hot chocolate ready for us?"

"I love you, Lish," he said, not answering the question, just looking at his daughter with an overwhelming fondness.

"I love you too, Dad."

"You want to sing a song?"

"Sure, I've got the perfect one! It's about family, you know the one." She smiled, he winked, and so they did.

EPILOGUE

Alicia stood on the small beach on the other side of the lake, looking wistfully into the woods beyond. Somewhere out there, she imagined a deer, a squirrel, and a noisy jaybird all watching out for each other. And she remembered a giant friend who made the ultimate sacrifice to save her and the lands he called home. She missed them all.

Suddenly, she squealed in surprise as cold lake water splashed against her back! She turned and saw her mother, Katie, cupping her hands in the water, ready for a second throw.

"Oh, no you don't," she warned and spun toward her mother, her hands raised like menacing, exaggerated claws just like one of her favorite monster movie villains, The Creature from the Black Lagoon. Alicia continued in character, stomping big stomps into the lake, water splashing high from each step.

Katie grabbed Alicia under the arms and spun her around. "You're almost getting too big for me to do that anymore!" she exclaimed, burrowing her face into the young girl's neck and making loud chomping noises against her skin.

"Stop, stop, STOP," Alicia laughed, screaming with delight. She squirmed away from her mother's grasp and threw herself into the water, swimming toward Richard.

"But you're not too big yet for me to throw you from my shoulders!" he said, laughing in response to the antics of Alicia and Kate. He ducked down into the water and Alicia clambered up onto his back, pulling herself higher until she planted her feet firmly on his shoulders. Her dad reached up, grasped each of her ankles, and then flexed his legs upward jumping into the air while releasing his grip which propelled Alicia through the air. She landed with a great splash nearby and came up choking from a combination of lake water and laughter.

Katie swam up to the two of them and looked at Alicia, smiling and said, "I love you,

you know."

"I know, Mom," she replied. These were the moments Alicia cherished with her parents. Now that she was a getting older, they didn't happen all that often. It made her happy that they seemed to have as much fun doing these silly things as she did.

"Hey, what about me?" Richard asked, feigning disappointment. "What am I, chopped liver?"

"I love you too, honey," her mother replied.

"Me too!" exclaimed Alicia. "Now let's swim. Dad, will you throw me from your shoulders again?"

"Sure," her father said with a smile.

Alicia turned back once more toward the woods. Did she see a flash of something? Something just at the periphery of her vision?

She squinted, shaded her eyes from the sun with her two hands, and looked closely, a golden mantled squirrel stood on its hind legs atop a log gazing at her intently. As she watched the squirrel, deciding this person didn't have any treats for it, dropped to all fours, scampering away into the bushes and out of sight.

Alicia turned back toward her parents, waiting patiently for their watery shenanigans to end, and felt a surge of gratitude for what she had. Life was good.

Mickey gazed out from the forest edge and watched the young girl at play with her family. He was sorry that he could not talk to her, but just seeing her made him happy.

"I CAW guess she made it back home after CAW all." Briar screeched. "What a CAW wonderful family. She looks so happy!"

"Yes, she does, Briar. She certainly does,"

Mickey replied, with a bit of sadness in his voice.

"Oh, CAW-ome on. She was never meant for our world," said Briar.

"You're right, I know." Mickey continued to look at the human child who, for a short time, had been a true friend. "I sure will miss her," he said with resignation.

"Me too, CAW, me too! Now can we go find some berries? I'm CAW starving!"

"Fine, shut your beak, you noisy bird. Do you want to attract foxes?" Mickey scolded the jay.

"I'm not worried about CAW foxes," Briar exclaimed as they turned back toward the dark woods and Fiona grazing just a few feet away. "I'll beat them off, just CAW like last time!" he bragged as he flew in and around the branches above. "Besides, we have Fiona. She doesn't

CAW talk much, but she sure can CAW kick!"

Mickey climbed up onto Fiona's shoulder and together, this oddball family moved off into the forest. With a backwards look and his eyes steamy with tears, he watched Alicia play until they were out of sight.